MAX'S CAMPERVAN

RESOLUTIONS AND Executions

TYLER RHODES

Copyright © 2025 Tyler Rhodes

All rights reserved. This book or any portion thereof may not be reproduced or used in any manner whatsoever without the express written permission of the author except for the use of brief quotations in a book review.

This is a work of fiction. Names, characters, businesses, places, events and incidents are either the products of the author's imagination or used in a fictitious manner. Any resemblance to actual persons, living or dead, or actual events is purely coincidental.

Dedicated to Alexis. Love you.

Chapter 1

"...and do you, Max Effort," the vicar paused as a few sniggers were badly stifled, so I took a moment to turn and smile at Min, knowing I had a gormless expression on my face but not caring.

"You look beautiful," I whispered.

"Thank you." Min smiled, her dimples making her cheeks resemble two rosy peaches, her face flushed with excitement and anticipation.

The vicar dabbed at her eyes, which had been streaming the whole day, then sneezed loudly. "Sorry, my allergies are playing up terribly today. It's all the pollen." She sneezed again and dropped her tissue. She retrieved it quickly, then mumbled, "Excuse me, I need to get a fresh one." Without pausing to ask if we minded her interrupting the ceremony, she rushed to the very battered and unsightly static caravan and disappeared inside. It was the only usable building at the rundown campsite, but she hadn't minded.

"We're going to be married," I teased, winking at Min.

"If she ever comes back. I can't believe she left when you were about to say I do." Panic arose in her eyes as Min gasped and asked, "You were going to say yes, weren't you?"

"You'll have to wait to find out," I laughed.

There was a rather awkward silence, as it wasn't normal to have your wedding interrupted like this, but then, this wasn't exactly a conventional wedding.

Anxious barked from behind us, and I turned to the little guy quivering with excitement in his penguin suit.

"What's the holdup?" shouted Dad. "Where's that woman gone? And she's not a proper vicar anyway. She's wearing Crocs. Should be illegal. You'd never get that in my day."

"So is everyone else, including you," I said quietly. Shouting felt wrong, even though we weren't in a church, but it was standard practice for my parents.

"Yes, we wanted it to be informal," agreed Min. "Everyone wearing Crocs and their summer clothes. Shorts and vests and ready to enjoy the weather and have a fun night camping." Min smiled warmly at me, her joy radiating, and I felt like the happiest man alive. After divorcing two years ago, then finally getting my act together after a year of madness as we went our separate ways, we decided we were destined to be together but took almost a year to confirm that we were doing the right thing.

Now here we were, finally about to make it official, and had chosen to do so at a campsite rather than in a church or registry office. It hadn't exactly gone to plan, and the site a few miles away we were supposed to use, one of our all-time favourite spots, had closed at unbelievably short notice because of family issues so we'd had to hurriedly change venue without having the time to visit in advance. When Min and I arrived the day before, we were shocked by what we'd discovered, but decided to make the most of it and now here we were itching to make our marriage official then have a great fun party with friends and family.

"I'm not wearing Crocs!" squealed Mum. "Don't you go telling everyone I'm a crime against fashion like you pair. It's not right. Min, don't you feel underdressed?"

"I'm wearing a white pair of shorts and vest and matching footwear. I'm overdressed, if anything," she giggled.

"Well, I'm not!" Mum twirled, showing off her cream dress with arresting blue polka dots in her usual fifties fashion with a blue bandanna, bright red dyed hair, flawless make-up, and matching blue high heels that sparkled in the sunshine.

"You look stunning, love," said Dad, beaming at her then turning his attention to Min and me. He looked us up and down, frowned, then grinned and added, "So do both of you. We're so happy."

"We really are. You make a lovely couple," conceded Mum, dabbing at her eyes, obviously fit to burst with pride and love.

"If they ever manage to get married. Where's the vicar? What's her deal?" asked Dad. "It's not right to be running off just as you're about to make your vows. Very unprofessional."

"Her allergies are really bad. It's the pollen," I said.

"Only because they haven't cut the grass and everything's so overgrown. This place needs a good tidy up." Dad scowled as he spread his arms to encompass the whole site.

We, along with the rest of the guests, meaning Anxious, looked at the strange campsite we'd ended up at and mumbled our agreement after checking the owners weren't around. Dad was right. The place had certainly seen better days. The fields weren't mowed, and in fact I'd had to borrow their ride-on mower to cut the grass where we were having the service and where we'd erected the large bell tents we'd thankfully rented.

The site was beautiful, that was obvious, but wasn't actually a functioning campsite despite me being able to book it. There had been a lot of confusion but I'd got everything sorted and set up in the end, so now all we had to do was actually get married and have a fun afternoon and evening with my folks, Anxious, and, most importantly of all, the love of my life, Min.

Large ancient trees swayed on a gentle gust that drifted past before all was still, the air heavy with pollen from surrounding fields full of crops, the long grass gone to seed, and wild flowers in the adjoining meadow and skirting the hedge lines of this little hidden gem of a place. Despite its shortcomings, Min and I had fallen in love with Craven Oaks Campsite the moment we'd arrived, stressed and panicked about if we'd be able to get married at all.

The perfume was more arresting than walking into Mum's bathroom after a trip to Boots, the air heavy with sun, birds chirping, and bees buzzing. That early summertime when the world feels full of hope, with the promise of warm days ahead for months and you find it hard to believe that wet, drab, cold, and short winter days could possibly be a thing in the same country.

"Isn't it so beautiful though?" said Min, seeming to get happier by the minute despite the pause in the ceremony. She looked so light I wouldn't have been surprised if she'd begun to float away like a dandelion seed on a tickling breeze.

"Not as beautiful as you." I kissed Min's cheek, feeling like I was about to explode with joy.

"Hey, no kissing until the vicar says so," warned Dad with a wag of his finger.

"Sorry," we chorused, then giggled and held hands.

"That's better." Dad crossed his arms and winked at me, as euphoric as the first time Min and I got married.

"We were lucky they let us have the wedding here, and I think we did a great job," said Min.

"We sure did. What better place than this? It's rather wild, and a bit rough around the edges, but it's a perfect spot."

"The hills look incredible with the sheep everywhere, there's a proper wild wood surrounding the site full of oak and beech and even hazel, a stream by the fence, the pretty flowers, and even the old barns are cute."

"I'm not sure cute is the word I'd use, but they do fit with the overall vibe," I sniggered, glancing away from her to the collection of old stone outbuildings and a large barn made when the house was constructed back in the sixteen hundreds and about as full of character as the lovely elderly couple who owned the place and had lived here for over half a century.

"I think it's adorable. And they were so kind to let us set everything up, even if you did have to do the mowing."

"It was very nice of them. Shame they had to close the campsite a few years ago. But I understand it's too much for them now." I glanced at the static caravan, wondering why the vicar was taking so long.

"And did you see the house? How amazing is it?"

"Yes, so amazing that they live in a single room at the back, because the rest of it is ancient and falling to bits. They don't even have central heating!"

"Max, you're a fine one to talk. Our entire home is smaller than that room by miles, and at least they have a toilet."

"True," I conceded.

A car screeched to a halt. I presumed they were up at the oak gate which was out of sight, while we were down in this little hidden area. A voice called out, "Hello?"

"Down here, Ernie," shouted Dad, then with a nod to me he rushed up the track and was gone.

A moment later he and Uncle Ernie came back, Ernie looking red from the rushing, his usual trilby perched atop his short grey hair, his slim figure suited but not quite booted in the two-tone style the ska nut adored. Black drainpipe trousers, white Fred Perry polo shirt, and cheery red braces completed a look only marred by him actually following the dress code at least partially and sporting a pair of brand new black Crocs.

"Sorry, so sorry. I got stuck behind a tractor for an hour because there was nowhere to overtake, then there were these stupid traffic lights every few miles and half were broken and stuck on red and nobody knew if they could risk trying to go past or not. Did I miss it? It's over, isn't it? What a nightmare. And my beautiful wife couldn't make it because her sister's poorly. I told you that on the phone, right?" Uncle Ernie removed his hat and rubbed at his head, then replaced it just as Anxious leapt into his arms, tail wagging merrily, super excited to see Uncle Ernie.

"You made it just in time," I said, slapping him on the back. "And yes, you told us."

"Wow, great! I get to see you guys get hitched at last. About time. Hey, your hair's grown a lot, and the beard's looking fine, Max. So glad I made it in time. Um, when does it start?"

"It already has," said Min, kissing his cheek.

"Huh? I don't get it."

Ernie released Anxious as I explained about the vicar going to get a tissue, and we turned to look at the unsightly green, white, but mostly just filthy static caravan. We waited, then waited some more, but she still didn't return.

"She must have needed to use the loo," said Uncle Ernie, puzzled. "Are vicars allowed to poo at weddings?"

"No, they aren't!" wailed Mum, looking concerned before kissing Uncle Ernie's cheek and frowning at his Crocs, her lips down turned.

"I guess she did need the loo," I agreed. "But it's bad timing as I was just about to say I do."

"Be a shocker if you said anything else," he laughed. "This is weird, though, right? I get needing a tissue if her allergies are playing up, but how long would that take?"

"Let's give her a moment, then I'm sure she'll return." Min took my other hand and it was like there were only the two of us in the whole world. With her blond hair waving as she moved, her smile a permanent fixture, her tanned slim body glowing with vitality, Min oozed happiness and had done so for the entire fortnight since she'd asked me to marry her. I was the same.

"It's been an incredible two weeks," I whispered. "The best ever."

"It has, hasn't it? Truly incredible. I thought it would be harder than it was with us living in Vee, but it's been perfect. Giving up work was the best thing I ever did. Besides asking my hunky fella to marry me again."

"We've had some amazing adventures, right?"

"Sure have. And no murders. Just you, me, and Anxious enjoying ourselves. I feel like I'm on a permanent holiday. Being at those wonderful campsites, even wild camping, and the beaches. Waking up in the morning is such a joy as I don't have to do anything or go anywhere, just enjoy being free and living an outdoors life. I love it."

"I'm so glad. I was worried you'd hate it and change your mind."

"You were?"

"A little," I admitted. "It's a massive change of everything, and I know it can take a while to adjust. It's nothing like living in a house and going to work every day."

"That's what I adore about it. Besides being with you and Anxious, of course. Stepping out into a new place to explore, feeling connected to nature, long walks every day, cooking outside, all of it. It's the best thing I ever did and I don't regret it at all. I know I still have the house to sort out properly, and there are loads of things to arrange, but this is the life for me."

"Min, I'm so happy. Now if that vicar would get a move on, we can make this official."

"It's getting super weird now, isn't it? We're chatting away in the middle of our wedding."

"And we can hear everything you're saying," teased Uncle Ernie. "You do know we're here, don't you?" He winked at me, his carefree attitude always something I looked forward to.

"We got caught up in each other. Sorry." Min smiled at everyone and added, "Hopefully we'll be married soon. Sorry for the delay."

"Don't you worry about it, love," said Mum. "You were meant to be together, so no need to get stressed."

Min nodded, then looked at me, a frown slowly forming.

"I'm sure everything is fine. She's just gone to the loo. The poor thing is a mess. Hayfever is exhausting and really takes it out of you. She'll be back in a moment."

We waited, but still she didn't return, the only sound the birds and bees and the wind gently tugging at the tree canopy. The sun beat down, intense and arid, early June already sweltering. I began to get uncomfortably hot as stress began to rear its ugly head. I'd been so relaxed ever since Min and I had agreed to resume our relationship, but we still weren't officially together until we got married.

That was the deal we made. She'd stayed over most nights, but until things were official we'd agreed she wouldn't actually move in properly. It had been glorious, though, with her ending up staying with me and Anxious much more than we were apart. We both ached to make it permanent, and from today it would be. We'd already sorted out Vee, my, now our, beloved 67 VW Campervan, the tiny amount of space an issue as always, but I'd got rid of everything I didn't absolutely need so she had if not plenty of room then enough to make it feel like her home as much as mine and Anxious'.

"That's it! I've had enough of this." Dad rolled up the already rolled sleeves of his pristine white T-shirt, hitched up his Levi's 501s — a new dark indigo pair especially for the occasion — flexed his biceps, then marched over to the dilapidated grubby monstrosity, his Crocs flapping at the heel.

"Dad, don't say anything rude. I'm sure there's an explanation."

"I'll give her an explanation!"

"What does that mean?" I wondered, smiling as he panic ran his steel comb through his hair.

"Never you mind." Dad pocketed his comb, rubbed his hands down his T-shirt like he was worried he'd get scolded by the vicar for being unruly, then rapped on the door. "Open up in there! You've only done half a wedding. Max and Min are desperate for some bedroom action, and they've been waiting until they're married like good kids."

"Dad, too much information," I warned, shaking my head in wonder at the depths of his lack of knowing what was and what wasn't appropriate to share with either a vicar or anyone else.

"Jack!" warned Mum. "You can't talk to a vicar that way. Vicars don't do that sort of thing."

"Don't they? I thought they did."

Mum shrugged, as close as she'd ever got to admitting she might possibly be wrong about something, then warned, "You mustn't talk that way. And don't knock so loud. It's disrespectful. You might make Him angry."

"It's not a him, she's a her." Dad grumbled under his breath, most likely something he knew Mum wouldn't appreciate, then turned to me and asked, "That made sense, right?"

"I think so," I lied.

"I meant Him. The big guy." Mum pointed to the sky then made the sign of the cross. "You have to be nice."

"Since when are you religious?" asked Dad. "And I doubt God is bothered about me knocking on a door. Right, that's it! This is getting daft." He turned the handle and the door creaked open. Squaring his shoulders, he stepped inside, calling out, "Are you decent? You shouldn't be naked in the middle of a wedding, though, and I can't think of any reason why you would be. Hello? Are you having a poo?"

"Jack, you stop that this instant," roared Mum, aghast. "Vicars don't poo. I already told you that. Especially lady vicars."

"Yes they do. Hello? Are you naked in the bedroom? Are you getting changed because of the pollen?"

"Stop telling the vicar she's naked," wailed Mum. She hurried over to us and tugged at Min's vest. "She wouldn't be, would she? Not when you haven't done your vows."

"Of course she won't be," said Min with the patience of a saint.

"This is turning into a really fun wedding, isn't it?" I sighed, wishing we could get on with things and for it to go smoothly rather than turn into what felt like a dodgy sitcom from the late seventies.

We turned as Dad clattered about inside, presumably checking the few rooms, then all went quiet.

Finally, he popped his head out of the doorway and with a confused look said, "Um, guys, sorry to tell you this, but I think somebody stole the vicar."

Anxious whined, then gave me a knowing look as if to say, "Here we go again."

Chapter 2

"I knew it!" hissed Min, stamping a foot.

"Hey, it's alright. I'm sure there's a simple explanation."

Anxious barked, then lay down and put his paws over his eyes.

"Max," sniffed Min, "it's just not going to happen, is it? It's like the world is against us and we're never going to be married. First the campsite closing, us nearly missing out on having somewhere to hold the wedding and party, and now the vicar's vanished. Everything's going wrong."

Min flung herself at me and I wrapped my arms around her petite frame, my six one versus her five five meaning she sobbed into my chest.

"Everything will be okay. Dad's probably not even checked properly. Let me go and have a look."

Min pulled away and with hope in her eyes said, "Yes, good idea. Maybe she's in there somewhere."

With a nod, I hurried over to Dad who was standing outside the "building" of sorrow, rubbing at his furrowed brow.

"Son, this is beyond weird even by your standards. Why would someone nab the vicar right when she was in the middle of your wedding?"

"Are you sure she's not inside? Did you look in every room?"

"There's only the bedroom and bathroom."

"It's a two-bedroom home."

"Oh! Right, then maybe she is inside. But she didn't call out."

"Let me check." With Anxious by my side, I stepped up into the ancient static caravan and ducked inside. The little guy ran down the galley kitchen and through an open door, so I followed, trying my best to ignore the dodgy smell and the cluttered, chaotic space.

The owners had cleared a few things out so the vicar could use it to get things ready, but all that amounted to was them clearing stuff off the kitchen counter and piling it up in the compact living room next to the built-in L-shaped sofa beside the dining table.

Anxious yipped from the bedroom, so I took a quick glance around the open-plan space, confirmed the vicar wasn't lurking behind the now retro orange sixties curtains, then followed the noise. Anxious was sitting on the unmade bed, the mattress rather gross and stained from a leak in the ceiling, his head cocked and tail wagging.

"I don't think you deserve a biscuit for finding a bed," I laughed.

He whined, then hopped down and sat facing the wardrobe. A sharp bark, and his hackles raised, gave me pause, and instantly I imagined the worst. Would somebody have killed the vicar and stuffed her inside? If so, how did they leave without being spotted? Windows. Duh!

I realised I was holding my breath, so tried to relax and slow my heart whilst breathing in and out to a count of five, then before I changed my mind I yanked open the door and jumped back, ready for who knew what. Falling onto the bed, and with Anxious now going spare, I fought with my surprisingly light attacker and managed to fling them off with a yell of, "Geddof me!"

"Who's hurting my Max?" screamed Mum as she, Dad, Uncle Ernie, and Min bustled into the small room, taking up so much space Mum and Dad had to join me on the bed.

I stared down at the old brown dress lying on the floor in a crumpled heap and laughed nervously. "It was just a dress that fell off a hanger," I gulped, burning up because the room was stifling and my nerves were frayed.

"You thought it was going to be a killer, or a dead vicar, didn't you?" laughed Uncle Ernie. "You and your murders. You're obsessed."

"I am not obsessed, and I'll have you know there hasn't been a murder mystery for weeks."

"Which means you're past due," he said, picking up the dress and hanging it up in the otherwise empty wardrobe.

"He's right, Max." Min chewed at her lip as our eyes met. "It's been ages since the last murder, and that's not good. Um, I mean it's good nobody died, but not good as this is meant to be our happy day and now someone has killed the vicar."

"Nobody has hurt the vicar. Can everyone please get out? It's too hot. We're sweating buckets."

They retreated to the main space while I followed behind.

"What's the plan, Son?" asked Dad.

"I'll check the other rooms, then we'll see. Everyone please wait here." The tiny bathroom was empty apart from a shampoo bottle on its side in the green shower cubicle. The liquid had oozed through the open lid and made a congealed pool. Something awful was growing on it. It waved at me as I backed out.

The other bedroom didn't even have a bed in it and had been used to store old furniture that was either broken or infested with woodworm. Why it hadn't been thrown away, I had no idea, but one thing I was sure of after searching the wardrobe and checking the room thoroughly was that it didn't contain a vicar.

Back out in the main room I shook my head, then we opened every door and checked under every piece of furniture, even in the fridge; Natasha was gone. No vicar for us. Which meant…

"No wedding!" Mum wailed, then flung herself down onto the sofa dramatically and beat it with her fists, coughing as dust billowed.

"Max, what are we going to do?" asked Min. "This is our special day. Do you really think someone took her?"

"I honestly don't know. I'm not sure of anything anymore. Where are her things? We need to find them, and her. Did anybody see anyone else around here today?"

"Her things are under your mother," said Dad. "She's hitting them right now." He moved to Mum then calmed her and helped her to sit up, then retrieved the brown canvas backpack the rather unconventional vicar had arrived with, saying it was all she needed. Rather than a black shirt and white collar, she wore regular summer clothes consisting of cream linen trousers and a lemon yellow blouse that made her jet black bob haircut and heavy dark eye make-up all the more arresting.

Easy to laugh, and with a warm smile, we took to Natasha instantly when we'd met her, especially once she explained that she would wear the collar if we wanted, but it wasn't necessary. The main thing was that she was qualified to marry us, and that was all we wanted.

"Open it then," urged Uncle Ernie. "We might find some clues."

"Ooh, goodie," crooned Mum, her upset forgotten as Dad unbuckled the backpack.

"Oh no you don't," I warned. "This is not some madcap mystery you get to solve. The vicar, Natasha, has just had a call or something and vanished. Most likely, she rushed out and nobody noticed. We weren't all watching the door."

"Yes, Son, whatever you say," said Mum, a picture of innocence. All eyes turned to her and there were a few gasps, as never in my life had she ever taken an order, or a request. She was her own woman, with more than enough ideas of her own to never need anyone else's input on any topic ever. "Why are you staring at me?"

"No reason, love," said Dad, shaking his head as he glanced my way, as bemused and confused as me.

"So, what's inside?" asked Min, slipping her arm around my waist and smiling at me.

"Let's have a little look-see." Dad, about as diplomatic and considerate as Mum, simply upended the contents onto the sofa. "A dog collar, a water bottle, some Tupperware, clothes, and look, a purse." Dad snatched it up and pulled out cards and cash, then his eyes raised and met mine.

"What's wrong?"

"Where exactly did you say you found this vicar?"

"I called around the area and Natasha was the name I was given. She holds sermons at several churches every week and does the weddings around here. Why?"

"Because whoever that was marrying you, and who has now vanished, was not Natasha Green."

"What are you talking about, you silly man?" Mum snatched the purse from Dad and the card he was holding fell onto the sofa. We crowded around as she picked it up and declared, "That's not the vicar. Why does it have her name on it?"

"Because she's an imposter," I sighed, feeling Min's arm tighten around my waist.

"Why does it have the vicar's name on the driver's licence but not her face? Someone's impersonating her? I don't get it."

"Mum, the woman we met is not Natasha Green. The woman on the licence is. Whoever this lady was, she was impersonating the vicar."

"But I spoke to her, and arranged for her to come and marry us," protested Min. "Why would someone pretend to be her? And does this mean we wouldn't have really been married?"

"I think it might, but I have no idea what is going on here. Let's go outside where it's cool and have a think about this. Dad, is there a phone or anything else that might help us figure this out?"

"There are a few bank cards and some notes, but nothing else. And no phone. Just sandwiches. Cheese and pickle, I think." He sniffed the open Tupperware and nodded. "Yep, definitely Cheddar and Branston pickle. Nice." Dad's eyes glazed over and he went to take a bite before Mum snatched it away from him. "Hey, why did you do that?"

"Bring out the Branston," everyone chorused, unable to help ourselves as it was the go-to pickle for most of the UK.

"You can't eat the vicar's sandwiches."

"But she isn't the real vicar."

"It doesn't matter. What if they're poisoned?"

"Why would they be?" Dad's eyes widened as he lowered the container onto his lap, eyeing the limp sandwich with distrust.

"Who knows? But you leave it alone." Mum replaced it, then closed the lid.

I took Min's hand and led her outside. Anxious sat waiting patiently and cocked his head, clearly wondering what was going on.

"Hey, buddy, thanks for waiting. Sorry about this, but it seems like that nice lady might have been an imposter. Not who we thought she was. We need to find her. Think you can help?"

I'd overdone it, so he simply wagged his tail.

"I have an idea." Min ducked back inside once everyone else came out, then returned with the lightweight summer scarf from the bag. She bent beside Anxious and suggested, "Track the scent. There's a biscuit in it for you."

That was all the incentive the keen tracker needed. He sniffed the scarf thoroughly, then began zig-zagging back and forth towards the static home before hopping up the steps and snorting his way inside. I followed behind, but kept back so he could do his thing. It was different to the last time we went in, as now he had a job to do, and I watched as he worked his way around the living room area then the kitchen before going first into the main bedroom then the spare room. When he didn't come back out, I crept forward and watched from the doorway.

Anxious was pawing at the floor, and whining quietly, then his head snapped around when he heard me and barked once; his work was done.

"What have you found, boy?" I wondered.

He scratched at a clear patch of cheap pine floorboards the same as in the rest of the small building. Most of the room was covered with furniture and random objects, but this part was clear.

Squatting beside him, it was obvious there was a rectangle cut out of the boards, so I pulled out my penknife and managed to slide it into the cut line disguised between the boards and pressed it up enough to get a hand under then flipped up a hinged trapdoor.

Anxious jumped into the hole without pause, brave as only the entirely innocent could be, then vanished. A moment later, I heard him bark outside and everyone gasp, then he clattered his way across the floor and entered the room again before sitting beside me, wagging happily, eyes glued to my pocket.

"Well done, buddy. You're so smart." I handed over a biscuit which he took gently then trotted back outside to enjoy his snack in the sunshine.

Intrigued by Anxious' vanishing act, everyone once again crowded into the room and stared at the hole in the floor.

"At least we know how she got out," said Min. "The only question is why? And who is she really?"

"A great question," said Dad, patting Min's head.

"Two questions, actually, and please don't pat my head."

"Did I do something wrong?" asked Dad, looking concerned.

"Jack, you can't pat a lady's head," snapped Mum, slapping his hand. "It's insulting, and apart from anything else you'll mess up Min's hair. It looks so lovely too."

"It really does." Dad smiled, trying to ingratiate himself, and Min laughed it off. Dad wasn't being condescending, he simply wanted to show affection and thought nothing of it.

"I better check it out," I told Min, winking at her, a knowing smile on her face assuring me she wasn't angry with Dad and that she was keen to figure this out as much as me.

I lowered myself into the hole and stood on the bare ground underneath, up to my waist beneath the floor. With no other choice, I got onto all fours then crawled around under the static caravan, raised up on blocks to level it. There was barely enough room to move, but I could see well enough to make out a line of scuffed earth where it looked like someone had been dragged out. Two deep furrows in the still slightly damp soft earth making me believe that our mystery fake vicar's heels dug in as she was pulled away. Or maybe she'd left of her own free will. It was hard to know for certain.

I emerged behind the building and stood then brushed myself down, scanning for any sign of fake Natasha or her kidnapper if that's what had happened. There was nothing, and I might have been mistaken. Maybe the marks were just her getting out, and when I ducked back under and checked the marks I'd made it was obvious that she might have crawled out herself.

When I returned to the others at the front of the building, it was to find Dad hugging Min, and Mum and Uncle Ernie looking concerned. Min was a strong, independent woman, but this was a lot to take in, and utterly unexpected and downright concerning. Whatever the reason for this woman impersonating the vicar, it didn't bode well. Not only had she pretended to marry us, she hadn't even finished the job, and now she'd either run off part way through the ceremony or been taken for reasons unknown.

I explained what I'd found, then said I'd go and see if I could follow the trail, so while Mum shoved Dad out of the way and wrapped Min in her arms, I called for Anxious and together we returned to the back of the building and began our search. We were nestled down in an enclosed area here, a secluded private space with the static caravan backing onto a thin strip of woodland. We followed the trail up to the fence line and Anxious ducked through a gap in the rusty metal, nose to the ground. I was tall enough to step over, so followed the little guy, noting a few snapped twigs on low thin branches of saplings, the leaf litter disturbed for a while until finally we emerged up near the entrance to the campsite, a little past the house, where the woods turned to boggy ground with scrubby grasses. It was dry now, but would be a quagmire in the winter.

There was no sign of anyone or anything untoward, but with direct access to the track approaching the site, and being around the bend from the house, it would be easy to get in and out unseen if you timed it right. But why bother? Why would any of this happen at all? None of it added up, and it certainly seemed like a lot of trouble to let us get half-married. Was it somebody who really didn't want me and Min together again? A prank possibly? Someone who had thought it was a clever idea to impersonate the vicar, then had second thoughts and couldn't go through with it? Why on earth would you do that in the first place though?

With nothing to gain here, we returned to the others. I explained everything, then we retreated to the large marquee we'd erected the day before where a table was loaded with food for lunch and plenty of drinks in the coolboxes for the afternoon when it would be just us before the party got going in the evening. We'd both agreed that a quiet ceremony would be nicest, keeping it intimate and taking the pressure off, but we'd invited friends for the evening and most had said they could make it. It would have been great fun, but now we weren't sure what to do. Should we cancel the whole thing? Call everyone and explain? Some might have already set off, and maybe this would be sorted out by then.

I couldn't help feeling optimistic, like somehow this would all be resolved, although I couldn't figure out how. But another part of me knew in my bones that this was another mystery that would take work and time to solve, and there was no way we could avoid it. For once, it was personal, and I was not happy about that at all or the upset this had caused.

"We'll solve this," I promised Min.

"I know we will," she said, resolute. "I'm not letting some fake vicar ruin our wedding day."

"Then we better get busy figuring this out."

"After we've had a glass of wine. I need it."

So it was settled. A quick drink, then we'd hunt down the mystery non-vicar and get some answers.

Chapter 3

My folks and Uncle Ernie agreed to wait at the marquee while we went up to the house to talk to the owners. Min had recovered and had a familiar set to her jaw, her shoulders squared, a "no-nonsense, I want answers," attitude locked in place. I was so proud of her, and myself, for handling this as well as we had. We didn't need to say anything; we were determined to get married no matter what.

"What if we can't get married today?" asked Min as we strolled up the field towards the house.

"We'll have to live in sin. That's what they called it back in the day, right?"

"It's too late for that. We were married for a long time."

"Does that mean tonight when we go to bed we can…?"

"You wish!" Min smiled, and squeezed my hand, but the look on her face made my stomach lurch and my heart beat fast.

"Wow, is it hot, or just me?"

"It's you and your filthy mind," she teased. "But seriously, Max, this is turning into a disaster. Not turning. It is."

"We can handle it. We've been through worse. As long as we're together, that's the main thing. How's it going with the house? I know you've been sorting through everything.

When I packed away my stuff to live in Vee, I was amazed how much I had, and that was after us already going through things and you keeping lots."

"It's going well. I gave tons to charity, sold some, and the rest will go into storage. I'm not saying I don't want to live in Vee with you guys, but it seems foolish to get rid of the furniture. Especially the items we both like."

"Makes sense. The main thing is we're together, wherever that may be."

"Actually, I got an offer."

"On the house? Already?"

"Already. I was going to wait and surprise you, but I hope it's okay and I accepted. It was well above the asking price, and they're a sweet couple. Max, the house made a fortune and in such a short space of time. I don't understand how anyone can afford to buy property now."

"How can this couple?"

"Because they moved out of London for her work, so to them it's cheap, but for us mere mortals it's an absolute fortune. It feels wrong to be making so much money off property as what hope is there for the younger generation?"

"They either stay at home with their parents, build a tiny home, or live in vans. It's why there are so many people taking up vanlife."

"It seems so unfair. I know prices were sky-high even when we bought our place, but nothing compared to now."

"I don't have the answers, but at least we know we'll be fine financially. Not that I'm saying you have to share the money," I added hurriedly.

Min pulled me to a stop and faced me. "That's what I wanted to talk to you about. When we got divorced, we shared things out. I got a house, you kept the rental properties, and the money in the bank was split, but we need to change that again. We should go back to joint accounts and joint ownership for everything, like the way it was."

"I was going to say the same thing, but wasn't sure you'd want to," I admitted. "I'm the one who ruined things, so I never want you to think that you'd come unstuck if…"

"That will never happen again. We both know that. Things are different now. We're different."

"You mean I am," I laughed.

"Yes, but so am I. Maybe getting divorced was the best thing that ever happened to us. It's led us to this, and a whole different future, so it worked out in the end. Um, apart from the fake vicar."

You had to see the funny side of it, and we both laughed at the absurdity of the situation. It was beyond ridiculous, yet our spirits had grown high now we'd calmed down, because there was no denying how much we enjoyed solving mysteries, no matter the dark side that always came with them.

What was so at odds with the peculiar day was how this place was affecting us. At first, it was a terrible shock to realise the campsite wasn't up and running and had been left to go rather wild, but as we wandered around and got busy sorting things out yesterday and this morning, we began to appreciate the magical qualities of it. Sometimes places feel special without understanding why at first. It's only when you take the time to really look, and open yourself up to your emotions, that you understand it's the flow of the land, the way a tree is positioned, or the meandering course of a babbling brook. Even where a house or outbuilding is sited can have a profound effect on the vibe, and combined, they add up to something magical and special.

"What was the name of this place again?" asked Min. "It's so lovely, and feels different to other campsites."

"Craven Oaks Campsite. The little town is called Craven Oaks, and sounds lovely. We'll have to visit."

"I like it! What does Craven mean? I've heard that before in town names."

"Apparently, it's probably from a Celtic word. Either garlic, or stony. Others think it means scratched or scraped. It's quite a mystery."

"So we're at Stony Oaks, or Garlic Place Oaks. I like Stony Oaks best."

"Me too, although there's masses of wild garlic in the woods, so maybe the town has lots of it around the area. Who knows?"

"All I know is it's magical. Come on, we better get a move on. A woman, whoever she was, has vanished, and she might be in trouble."

"Or the real vicar."

Our eyes widened and together we groaned.

"Oh no! Max, we must check. What if she's dead, or hurt, or in danger?"

"We'll have a word with the owners, then make some calls. Let's go."

Much as we would have liked to take our time and study the charming house, we had much more important business to attend to, so we skirted around to the side and opened the door to a lean-to style addition which was the only room they currently used. It had been professionally extended years ago, giving much more space, even built out of local stone like the rest of the building, and you'd never know it wasn't original.

Min rapped on the open door then we entered; standard practice in these parts and what we'd been told to do. Anxious went next, then I brought up the rear and shut the door behind me. Like the day before, it was stifling hot inside; they weren't big on ventilation.

What was markedly different was the number of suitcases, holdalls, and boxes stacked beside the sliding doors that gave incredible views over Craven Oaks town and countryside.

"Hello?" Min called out.

Anxious barked a hearty greeting, too, as the elderly couple adored him so he knew treats were likely.

The tap-tap-tapping of Carl's walking stick signalled his approach from the hallway through the open doorway, and he appeared a moment later with Maureen slowly walking behind him.

"It's the happily married couple," croaked Carl, his voice raspy from years of smoking—at eighty-nine he decided to give up and complained it was the worst decision of his life as now Maureen wouldn't let him start again.

"Did it go well?" asked Maureen, painfully craning her neck to look up, her hunched back clearly a source of trouble.

Both wore their usual house clothes, Maureen in a blue housecoat, fluffy slippers, and a pleated green dress. Carl with black chinos from Marks and Sparks, a farmer's style check shirt, woollen scarf, and fingerless gloves. Both had a sweat on, and were breathing heavily.

"There's been a slight hiccup," said Min, exchanging a glance with me. What had these two been up to?

"That's a shame. Anything we can do? You'll have to make it quick though, as we're off soon. Our son's coming to collect us, then it's away to Barnstaple for us. He's got a big van especially for the move."

"Move? What move? And you never said you were going to Barnstaple. What's there?"

Carl frowned and grunted, "Our son, of course."

"You're moving out?" I asked.

"Sure are. Didn't we say? We told you this place was too much for us now, and I thought I mentioned it."

"No, you didn't. Um, you're okay leaving with us still here?"

"Course we are, dearies," laughed Maureen. "We'll lock up this old place, but there's nothing worth taking anyway. Lots of stuff has already been sold or collected by our boy, and everything else will be left for the new owners."

"You've sold it?" I asked, feeling sad at the thought, although not sure why.

"Not yet, but it's going on the market in a few days. Unless you want to make us an offer?" Carl chuckled, which turned into a racking cough so severe that he had to hold on to the wall until it passed.

Min and I exchanged a look, and it was as if a spark of electricity passed through us. Could we? Should we? What about the life we'd planned? But I had been thinking about running a campsite for a while now, and even Dad had suggested it not so long ago. Min had also expressed an interest in living this kind of lifestyle, but now it suddenly felt like a real option.

"How much will it be?" asked Min, nodding to me and smiling weakly as chances are it would be well over a million.

"Not as much as we'd hoped. The estate agent said the whole interior needs gutting. New plaster, new electrics and heating, insulation, new windows, and even floors. That's why we just live in this room."

"And the fact we can't get up the stairs and the outhouse is just through the side door," corrected Maureen.

"True." Carl took her hand and they entered the extension, then both shuffled over to the ratty brown corduroy sofa and carefully eased down with a sigh of relief. "This is too much for us, and it's time for something different. A new adventure. We've loved our sixty years here, but it's time for someone to make a real go of things and get it up to the standard people expect nowadays. Needs a new toilet block and barns repairing, tons of work on the land, and don't get me started on the old lake."

"There's a lake?" I asked.

"A huge one up that steep path. Be perfect for glamping or whatever they call it. Used to attract fisherman too. They pay top money, but that was years ago. We had to stop as we can't get up there. I hate to think what it looks like now. Anyway, enough about that. What happened?"

"They want to know the price," hissed Maureen. "Tell them."

Carl nodded, then told us what it was valued at. He was right; it was very reasonable and less than Min had sold her house for.

"That's a fair asking price," I noted. "Are you sure the estate agent valued it correctly? You couldn't get more?"

"Max!" Min shook her head, but I saw the look of concern; she didn't want them to get ripped off either.

"No, it's correct. Our son said it was right too. He runs a removals company up north and said this price is lots more than it would be worth up there. If you knew what we paid for it sixty years ago, you'd understand why we're happy enough with it. We already bought a lovely bungalow up there with a nice big garden and even booked someone to come every week to tend to it. We might not be able to do much work any more, but we like to potter. It's going to be great for us. Near to our boy and the grandchildren and the great-grandkids."

"Then good luck to you both. We hope you'll be very happy. But are you sure it's okay for us to stay here without you? If you were leaving, you should have said."

"And let you miss out on your big day?" asked Carl. "That's not our way. You asked, and we were happy to have you. A final, fun event before we leave."

"That's the issue, I'm afraid," I said with a sigh. "We were halfway through the wedding when the vicar vanished."

Both laughed, but when they realised I wasn't joking Maureen said, "I think you better put the kettle on, Carl."

"I'll do it," I offered.

Once tea was made, we explained everything, and they listened with increasing amazement. When we'd finished, Carl told us that he'd installed the trapdoor fifteen years ago.

"Can I ask why?" I wondered.

"Fun for the grandkids. They liked to make dens underneath and scare the living daylights out of our son and our charming daughter-in-law. You should have seen their faces the first time it happened. They were white with shock."

"Like ghosts, they were," laughed Maureen.

"Who else knew about it?"

"Oh, everyone who stayed there. We always told people so they'd be careful. I'd totally forgotten about it, actually, as the old thing has seen better days and hasn't been rented out for years. The roof leaks and the power doesn't work, and it's full of junk."

"And do you know the vicar?" asked Min.

"Natasha is new. Only been the local vicar for ten years, or maybe less," noted Carl. "We don't go to church, so haven't met her. We keep to ourselves."

"So you don't know what she looks like?" I asked.

"Course we do. Likes to dress casual, hardly ever wears her collar, and has very black hair and is quite pretty, so we've been told. Lots of fun, and numbers are up at services. People like her."

"So this mystery Natasha we met looks like the real one. It was hard to tell from her photos, but it definitely wasn't her that we met. The hair is the same, but the face was different."

"Then it sounds like you have a real mystery on your hands. Good luck figuring it out. We wish we could help, but we have to go today as the van is coming."

"You get on with your move. What should we do with things here? As if it's alright, we'll still stay until tomorrow."

"You stay as long as you like. Unless," Carl licked his lips, "you want to make us an offer on the place? Save the estate agent fees and the hassle. And we'd prefer if it went to someone we like and trust. We can tell you're good people, and we like your history. It's so sweet."

"Can we mull it over? Give you a call later or tomorrow?" I asked.

"Max, seriously?" Min gripped my arm and her eyes sparkled with excitement.

"I'm just asking. Keeping options open. But right now we need to figure this thing out."

"You have our number. We might be old, but we know how to use smartphones, so send us a WhatsApp or just give us a call by the day after tomorrow as that's when we have to confirm things with the estate agent. Good luck, and we're so sorry things went wrong for you today. What a real head-scratcher. Never been anything like that here before."

"What are you talking about?" asked Maureen. "Of course there has. Remember back, oh, must be nine or ten years ago?"

"That was a misunderstanding," grunted Carl, looking away.

"It was not, you silly old fool. A man died."

"An unfortunate accident."

"Is it okay to ask?" Min nodded her encouragement to them.

Carl sighed, rubbed his thin white hair, and coughed to clear his throat. "It was a fishing accident. A man was in a rowing boat. Must have been drinking, and fell asleep. He drowned. We had the police here for days, and it caused no end of trouble. It was getting too much for us anyway, so after that we never re-stocked the lake or went up there again. Terrible business, but just an accident."

"It was so upsetting. His wife came all the way from Luton to see where he died, and she was very snappy with us."

"Love, it wasn't our fault. The boat was sound, but we can't watch people and stop them drinking. He should have known better."

"Anyway," said Maureen brightly, "it was years ago. Water under the bridge. You two find your vicar, and let us know what happens. It was lovely meeting you both, and your parents."

"That's very diplomatic of you," I chuckled, knowing Mum and Dad were an acquired taste.

We rose, said thanks once again, and it was only then that I realised Anxious had been unusually quiet, and I'd forgotten he was there. When I couldn't find him, I began to panic, then a familiar thumping of a tail gave the game away and his head poked out from a wicker basket beside the wood burner that was running on low despite the heat.

"I think somebody's already made themselves at home," giggled Maureen.

My eyes met Min's, and we smiled, then she called him and we left the couple to finish packing.

Chapter 4

"We need to find the real Natasha," whispered Min the moment we were back outside.

"The best bet is to check the church. That was where she said she was working from today. Remember?"

"That's right. She said she felt like an office worker sometimes when I spoke to her yesterday. That she had more paperwork than a secretary, and preferred to work from the church. Maybe that's where this other woman…"

"It's okay. You can say it."

"Where she possibly murdered her, or is holding her captive. Max, should we call the police?"

"Maybe. But it's probably quicker if we just go and check things out then call them afterwards. We better tell the others, and somehow convince them not to come with us."

"Good luck with that." Min stood on tiptoe and kissed me, her sad smile breaking my heart.

"It will be okay. We'll work this out, and we are getting married no matter what."

"And live happily ever after."

"Yes, exactly."

We followed Anxious along the worn path in the grass, then back down to our private camping field. My thoughts were like a washing machine, everything swirling around, colliding, but a jumbled mess. I had to let the cycle finish so they could be separated and I could straighten out the chaos and make sense of things, and to do that we needed more information.

We filled the others in on what had happened at the house, not that there was much to tell beyond the surprise the owners were leaving and selling the property.

"You should buy it," insisted Dad. "I told you before that once you two were married something like this would be perfect for you both."

"Yes, but it's a lot of responsibility, and so much work," sighed Min, glancing around at the serene forest wistfully.

"That's what you two thrive on. Hard work. A challenge. And like I told Max, you could still live in the van if you wanted. You could change pitches as often as you want, but have a permanent base. Whenever you wanted to, you could go off on trips, or live in tents, or make some glamping pods or have yurts. All that modern stuff."

"Jack's right," said Mum, frowning at being left out of the idea. "And if you insist on living in Vee, then you could rent the house out as a holiday home and charge a fortune. People pay so much to stay in nice houses at sites like this. It's a fantastic campsite. It feels magical."

"It does have something special about it," agreed Uncle Ernie.

"It's something to think about," I admitted, unsure if it was a good idea or would put too much of a strain on our brand new relationship. We'd spent time together and a lot more often since the divorce, but never for more than a few days at a stretch. Jumping straight into an almost overwhelming project like this was a massive ask and a decision not to be taken lightly. Still, it was tempting.

"Let's focus on what needs doing for now," said Min. "And that's solving this case. Everyone, do you mind waiting here while Max and I go to the church to see if we can find anything out?"

Anxious barked, looking annoyed.

"Yes, you can come, too, buddy," I confirmed.

"We can finish preparing for this evening," said Uncle Ernie. "You two go off. We'll get everything set up here."

"Are you sure?" Min glanced at the piles of poles and canvas still to be erected, the stacks of boxes containing food and drink, the unfolded tables, and more.

"Ernie's right," said Dad. "We'll handle things here."

"And have a nice glass of wine," said Mum, rubbing her hands together.

"It's not even lunchtime yet," I protested, knowing the last thing we needed was Mum getting plastered so early in the day, or at all.

"It's a special day."

"Not yet, it isn't," grumbled Dad. He realised his mistake and added, "But I'm sure Max and Min, and Anxious, will figure it out."

"Then we'll be as quick as we can," I told them, then we hurried over to Vee, sorted a few things out, including a picnic for lunch just in case, and headed off.

Once off the site, we bounced down the bumpy track, surrounded by fields and sheep, the rolling Shropshire Hills in the distance, the Long Mynd, Stiperstones, and endless other beauty spots within a short distance. You certainly could never tire of the scenery in this luscious part of the country. The West Midlands was a firm favourite with both Min and I, and we'd lived in the area for years, only a stone's throw from the Welsh border, with a beautiful mix of people and cultures. It was rural, yet afforded easy access to large towns and cities, and the ancient town of Shrewsbury was always a delight to visit.

What I always adored about staying here, apart from it being close to our old home and my folks, was that in an hour and a half you could be at the coast and visit Aberystwyth, Aberdyfi, or head up a little to Barmouth and Harlech, and the incredibly varied offerings at the huge Shell Island campsite, giving you the absolute best of both worlds.

The track to the campsite wasn't too rough, and soon we hit a proper narrow road that led down into the town, a quirky, small place with just a few streets, plenty of independent shops, cafes, restaurants, five pubs, which seemed excessive, and a weekly farmer's market. It had everything you needed, and all set against a backdrop of hills, far away from the hustle and bustle of city life. You never got traffic jams or endless motorway monotony as there were no motorways, just quiet country roads leading to another beauty spot.

"It's so gorgeous around here, isn't it? I never tire of looking at the countryside." Min sighed, and tucked her legs under her; Anxious was curled up in her lap, dozing, as content as always.

"It's the best place in the whole country. Shame the other campsite was closed, but at least we found somewhere."

"And it's even more stunning, anyway, so that part worked out fine. Max, what do you think we'll find?"

"I hope we'll find this fake vicar and there will be an explanation, but what I think we'll find is a whole lot of trouble."

"Me too!" Min giggled nervously, then shook her head, curls catching the dazzling light through the split-screen window of our beloved home on wheels. "Sorry, didn't mean to laugh. I guess it's nerves. And excitement. We've done it again, haven't we? Got caught up in a mystery and let the excitement build. It still feels wrong to not just be worried about people, but also keen to solve a mystery."

"And the same as always, we shouldn't be too hard on ourselves. Let's park around the back of the high street, then we can walk to the church and see if we can uncover anything."

The car park was half empty, a sign of how rural we were, but maybe late Saturday mornings weren't a busy time. Anxious was in his element, having a new place to explore, but behaved impeccably and kept pace with us, taking the middle so his two favourite people were by his side.

Nerves rose as we ascended the steps to the quaint church just off the high street set on a generous plot with gravestones circling the centred place of worship. It was older than most of the town, dating back to the twelfth century in parts, with the tower having been rebuilt as recently as the eighteenth century. Lichen-covered stone dazzled us with multi-coloured hues as sunlight glinted off the facade through the utterly oversized pines, their branches drooping as if to greet worshippers or mourners, casting long arms of shade like a comforting cuddle over parishioners and tourists.

The three generous stone steps were worn in the centre from centuries of footfall, and I wondered how many people had passed over the threshold, pushed on the thick, oak door studded with ironmongery, or tugged at the ring handle, worn as smooth as the stone by thousands of hands.

The door squealed as I pushed it open, the cool air rushing out to greet us, as if calling welcome, and inviting us inside to take sanctuary from the relentless sun pounding our heads. We both lifted our sunglasses to our foreheads, the low light levels welcome after the glare.

"It's extraordinary," gasped Min, eyes tracking up to the rather surprisingly ornate oak ceiling, where beams criss-crossed. The entire structure was overlaid with pine boards before the tiles were laid, thick stone slabs that must have weighed a ton.

"Very impressive. And look at the floor. You don't get workmanship like that nowadays."

"Look how small the tiles are, and in such pretty patterns. Wow! And check out the stained glass above the... Um, what's it called?"

"The pulpit?"

"No, that's over there." Min pointed to the left where a large, new oak lectern stood proudly on a raised step. "Ah, I know, it's the chancel isn't it?"

"I think that's the private part for the vicar, through that door I suppose, as there aren't any others. No, wait, I'm getting confused. A chancel is where the pulpit is. The vicar's private room is the vestry." For some reason, I felt proud of myself for remembering.

Despite the beautiful stained glass, the amazing floor, the strict regimented rows of pews, and the rather crumbling ancient lime plaster making the place feel timeless and like I should get down on my knees and pray, I gulped as my eyes lingered on the closed door to the vestry. What would we find behind it?

"Let's not mess about. Come on." Min grabbed my hand and marched over to the door, then released me and stood there, waiting. "Well?" A raised eyebrow was all the not-so-subtle hint I needed.

"You want me to open it? Don't you want to go first and be the one who saves the day?"

"Max, stop it! I'm freaked out enough without you teasing me."

"Sorry. Okay, maybe stand back and don't look until I give the all clear."

"I'm staying right here. I can handle it."

"If you're sure?"

"Positive."

We nodded, then I grasped the cold iron ring. After it turned stiffly, a clunk of metal against metal signalled that the latch was lifted. I eased it open a fraction, the hinges cringe-inducing as the squeal rang out and echoed around the silent, holy space.

"Here we go." With a deep breath, I flung the door open and we both gasped as we rushed into a simply furnished, but comfortable office type space with a large old desk with a green reading lamp, covered in papers and books. Oak bookcases held just a few ancient relics, the flagstone floor was covered in several faded rugs, and a filing cabinet looked incongruous against the historic setting, but that wasn't what caused us to rush forward and for me to check behind the door just in case we were about to be jumped.

Tied to a chair in the middle of the room was a woman with very black hair cut into a bob, a pretty face, wearing bright summer clothes, leaving her arms bare. Like something out of a cheap thriller movie, she was tied to the plain pine chair with rope. She was gagged with a scarf, a lemon yellow summer affair that complimented her matching sandals. The vicar's eyes widened in shock then relief when she spied us, then began rocking in the chair and straining at her bonds as she tried to talk through the gag

Anxious' hackles were up and he raced over to the woman, Natasha, I assumed, then sniffed around before barking and dashing to the only other door in the room where he scratched at the wood and whined.

"Okay, Anxious, just chill a minute. Let's get the vicar free," I told him. He sat and wagged, pleased with himself, so I helped untie Natasha while Min fiddled with the gag and finally got the knot undone.

"Thank you. Thank you so much!" Natasha shook out her arms then burst into tears, but she was clearly a strong-willed woman and brushed them away instantly, leaving wet smears on her forearms.

"What happened? Are you hurt?" asked Min.

"I'm okay. Shaken up, but unhurt. I don't understand any of this. It makes no sense."

"We can hear all about it later, but for now I want to know if there's anyone through that door," I said.

"Yes. No. Maybe. A woman tied me up, said she was sorry but she had no choice, then she left through the back door. But I doubt she's still there now."

"Nobody else was involved? You didn't see anyone?"

"No, just her. She took my clothes from my bag. I deal with a lot of young children so always have a change or two in there. What is happening? I don't understand. Do I recognise you?"

"We spoke yesterday. You were meant to be marrying us today," said Min.

"Of course. Yes. That woman, that horrid woman, she looked through my diary and then took it. It had my appointments in it. I have a backup online, but it was so strange."

"She didn't come back? Has she been here recently?"

"No, not for hours. What is this all about?"

"That's what we'd like to know. Let me check through the door. Anxious seems certain there's something on the other side. Where does it lead?"

"To outside. It's always locked, just like the other one, but that woman made me unlock them both."

Anxious was still sitting with his eyes fixed on the door, but glanced at me as I came beside him. With a nod to him, he stood, ready to defend us, so I turned the handle and flung it open then jumped back, my heart hammering, sweating despite the cool room.

Sunlight and heat poured in, but nobody attacked and nothing more menacing than a bee moved, so I poked my head outside, then hurried into the light and checked along the walls. We were alone.

I bent to my buddy and asked, "What's going on? What can you sense?"

He yipped, then yanked my bag, pulling out the scarf we'd found in the static caravan, then dashed off onto the grass and weaved between the gravestones.

"Hold on, buddy. Wait for me. It might be dangerous." I chased after him, mindful of the graves, many with fresh flowers, but he'd stopped beneath one of the massive pine trees and was already backing up.

"Who would do something like this?" I felt sick, and had to turn away quickly, then steeled myself and took in the terrible sight before me. The fake Natasha was tied to the tree, the rope going around and around like someone had got entirely carried away. Her arms were pinned to her sides, her legs ramrod straight and closed. The wig was askew, revealing a buzzcut of brown hair beneath.

Straight through her heart was what looked like a poker you'd use for the fire. It had a twisted, spiral handle in decorative loops, like ones I'd seen before at craft fairs and festivals. Something that could only be made by hand and by a blacksmith who knew how to bend the metal to his will.

The woman's eyes were wide open in shock and her teeth were bared, and poking out of her mouth was a length of red ribbon like an impossibly long tongue. It stretched down to her chest, and as I stepped forward, intrigued despite the horror show before me, I angled my head and read the white letters scrawled on the ribbon with some kind of marker.

"Liar," I read, then gasped as the body seemed to come alive for a moment. I jumped back, hit a gravestone, and landed flat on my backside. An angry squirrel screeched as it perched on her shoulder for a moment then shot up the tree and continued to call out in protest at its serene day being disturbed in such a grisly fashion.

Anxious went wild and raced to the base of the tree and barked up at the now chattering squirrel before it climbed high then jumped into another tree and was gone.

"I think you scared it off," I sighed. Anxious turned, a cheesy grin on his face, proud as anything, and wagged. "Yes, good job." I winced as I stood, then patted the dust off my shorts before inspecting the corpse again. There was nothing else to see, just the blood that had pooled at her feet and the line of red down her leg and the bloodstained summer shirt she'd stolen from Natasha.

I called for the little guy, then we rushed back inside where Min was helping Natasha to open a bottle of water she was having trouble with as her hands were shaking.

"Did you find anything?" asked Min. The moment she caught my eyes she gasped, her hand shooting to her mouth. "She's dead, isn't she?"

"She is. Pinned to a tree. Tied to it, actually. Someone rammed a poker right through her."

"What is going on here?" screeched Natasha. "The woman who tied me up is dead?"

"I'm afraid so. Now we have a real murder mystery on our hands." I rubbed at my face, then stroked my beard, the sensation a comfort, and wondered why on earth a woman would impersonate a vicar, disappear halfway through a ceremony, then be tied up and murdered right where she'd begun her peculiar activities.

One thing was for sure. I was going to find out. This was not turning out to be the perfect wedding day, but maybe it had been the perfect murder.

Chapter 5

"I better take a look," said Natasha.

"It's very gruesome. And sorry, we haven't been introduced properly. I'm Max, this is Min, and the little guy is Anxious."

"Aw, what's the matter, sweetie?"

I cursed under my breath for forgetting to add the usual disclaimer, but the stress had made me forget.

"It's not his emotional state, it's his name," said Min before I could.

Anxious sat and wagged, paw held up, whining.

"Don't fall for it. His paw is fine," I explained. "But he likes you."

"And I like you, Anxious. What a funny name." Natasha smiled as she squatted, but then gasped and shot upright. "Sorry, but I've been stuck in that chair for hours and it's playing havoc with my sciatica. I can't figure this out at all. Why on earth would she tie me up and why would someone murder her? And gosh, where are my manners? I'm Natasha, and it's so nice to meet you. I'm assuming the wedding didn't go as planned? It's such a lovely day for it too."

"Nice to meet you," said Min, before they shook hands.

"Yes, great." I shook her small hand. It was warm and soft; there was no wedding ring.

We explained quickly about the strange events of earlier, then I called the police and went through what had happened again, focus on the corpse, and was told to stay put and not to touch anything. After I hung up, I dashed outside, snapped photos, then returned to the others.

Natasha was making a cuppa over at a small counter that housed a kettle and mugs with a compact fridge underneath. She drank hurriedly, seemingly able to handle the scalding water.

"Can you tell us more about what happened?" asked Min. "The police will be here soon and then we won't get a chance to chat."

"Of course." Natasha played with the cross on her delicate gold chain, then closed her eyes and clasped her hands together. She said a silent prayer which seemed to calm her, as when she opened her eyes she was much more relaxed and smiling almost beatifically. "Ah, that's better. Always lifts the spirits when I have a quick chat with the Big Guy."

"That's what you call him?" I wasn't sure why, but the name surprised me.

"People call God by many different names. It doesn't matter. Faith, compassion, and understanding are what matters. But love is the most important. For your fellow man, for all creatures, and for yourself above all else. You can't truly love another unless you love yourself."

"Well said!" I laughed, liking her immensely.

"How did you get tied up? Was it awful?" Min patted Natasha's arm, full of sympathy, and she was clearly shaken as she almost burst into tears again.

"I… it… it was the strangest thing. It must have been about half eight this morning. I had a mountain of things to do before I came to marry you, so got here earlier than usual. A woman was waiting on the front pew. She said her name was Mary, and I said that was a coincidence as I knew a man who was very close to a Mary."

"Who's that?" I asked. When both women's eyebrows raised, I cleared my throat and held up my hands in apology. "Oh, right, that Mary."

"Yes. She laughed at my little joke, although I'm afraid I'm not the best at telling them. Anyway, she asked if she could have a word, said it was of the utmost importance. I didn't think anything of it and she seemed upset, so I said I'd make her a cup of tea in here."

"Did she seem nice?" wondered Min.

"Yes, very. A lovely smile, and easy to laugh. Her hair was very short, which isn't usual, but I didn't want to pry into the why. I made tea, we sat down, then she went quiet. We drank in silence for a while, then I asked if she'd like to tell me what was wrong. I'm afraid I might have been rather moody as I had so much to do, but the next thing I knew she'd begun to cry. I put my tea down and went over to comfort her, then she sprang to her feet, punched me, said sorry, then shoved me onto the floor."

"That's nuts. She did that to a vicar?" gasped Min.

"We are just people," laughed Natasha. "I'm a woman, and a Christian, but a regular person. I was so shocked I didn't have time to react, but as I lay there on the floor I asked her why she was doing this and offered her money if that was what she needed. She shook her head, said sorry again, then pulled a long line of rope from her bag and ordered me to sit in the chair. I did as she asked and she tied me up. After that, she looked through my diary, grunted and smiled when she found something, then asked, "They changed the venue?"

"She was talking about our wedding?" I asked.

"Yes. She demanded to know why it was changed and I told her what you, Min, had explained. She hissed, and wasn't happy, then closed my diary and put it in her bag along with some of my things. Then she apologised, and it seemed like she truly meant it, before she tied my scarf over my mouth and left. She went through the back door we just used, and I've been alone until you arrived. Thank you so much for coming. Who knows how long I would have been here otherwise?"

"We're glad we could help. Who do you think she was? What could she want? She didn't take anything of value?"

"Not my phone, but she did take my purse. Did you find it?"

"We did," said Min, "but I assume the police will want it and her bag as evidence. We have it in the van."

"That's something, at least. What a morning. I was so scared, and worried she might return and do something awful, but now it's her who has been killed."

"Has anyone else been asking questions or acting strange?" I wondered.

"Not that I can think of. I see so many people, and deal with many poor souls with issues, but no strangers and nothing different than usual."

"And this woman wanted to come to us?" asked Min.

"It seemed that way. She asked about the venue change."

"So she had something in mind for either us or one of our guests, but something happened and she vanished. Did she have hayfever when you saw her?"

"Why, yes, she did! Her eyes were streaming and she kept using a tissue. I suffer myself, but with tree pollen, so I'm usually just slightly sniffly at this time of year. The pine trees flower earlier."

"Any mention of the campsite? Could it be to do with that?"

"She didn't know you'd changed places until she read my diary. There was no hint the actual location was important, but then again, she wasn't in the sharing mood. Just wanted to be on her way."

"Did she ask about us by name?" I wondered.

"Um, she did, actually. She said Max and Min, then laughed. Said it was such a silly name. Mumbled something like, I guess I'll have to make a max effort myself. Sorry, but do you think you know this poor woman?"

"Absolutely not. We didn't recognise her, and have no clue who she could possibly be. It's beyond confusing. Why leave halfway through the ceremony?" Min gnawed at her lip, as confounded as me.

"Maybe she wanted to ensure you didn't get married. By disrupting things the way she did, it's stopped it happening, hasn't it?"

Min and I locked eyes and something seemed to click into place between us.

"That must be it!" screeched Min. "Someone wants to ruin our future and stop us ever being together."

"Min, there's nobody in our lives like that."

"There might be. Maybe it's one of the criminals you, or both of us, helped to put away. What if one of them has escaped, or their family has got it in for us? We wouldn't know what they looked like."

"Yes, but if that's the case, why then kill the poor woman pinned to a tree outside? If she was family of someone who hates us, why is she dead? That leaves us with even more questions than ever."

"You're right." Min deflated, and slumped into the chair, staring glumly at the bunch of rope at her feet.

"Is that paracord?" I asked, bending to scoop up the tangle of black and red rope. I tugged on it and it was rather stretchy. At only a centimetre thick, it was incredibly strong, and with it pulled taught around Natasha there was no way she could have ever escaped. It matched what was used outside, now I came to think of it.

"I have no idea what paracord is," admitted Natasha. "I'm a vicar, not an outward bounds kind of lady," she chuckled.

"They use it for guy ropes, and for mountaineering, abseiling, that kind of thing. You get different tensions and thicknesses, but it's super strong. Is there anywhere around here that sells it? It looks brand new."

"Just the camping shop, I suppose. It's up the high street."

"Then maybe we'll go and check it out. Just on the off chance."

"Won't the police do that sort of thing? Why would you do it?" Natasha reached for her tea, then gulped the rest. I left mine as it was cold.

"Max is rather an expert at solving murders. He's got his own wiki page and has quite a reputation. I help sometimes, and usually solve the toughest ones if I'm around." Min winked at me and had to stifle a laugh despite the gravity of the situation.

"Is this true? My, that's quite a calling."

I turned to her and asked seriously, "You think it is a calling? I know it sounds silly, but ever since I got my van and I began living in it full-time, it has felt like a calling. Wherever I go, I end up getting embroiled in a murder mystery. It's like I'm meant to do it."

Natasha clasped her hands together, and spoke directly to me, "Max, there are some people in this world who are singled out to do the bidding of a higher power. Now don't get me wrong and think I'm getting religious on you, but there is more to this world than any of us could ever possibly know. It sounds like this is your calling. That you roam so you can help others, aid communities, and as much as I hate the word, to give people closure. You're chosen."

"Thank you for saying that. It's nice to hear."

"We should make sure nobody sees the body," Min suggested.

"Good idea. We don't want anyone getting upset." Natasha smiled weakly, clearly exhausted by her ordeal, and shaken, although she was handling it well.

As we grabbed our things, the door banged closed and it was locked.

"Where did you leave the key?" I asked in a panic, trying the handle anyway.

"It's always left in the door. Wasn't it there when you arrived?"

"No. Maybe our mystery woman took it."

"She might have. I can't say I was paying much attention."

"And the key to the other door?" I asked, rushing over, but before I got there, it slammed shut and was locked.

We were trapped inside.

"The keys are both kept together. I unlocked and came in here with that woman, then she must have taken them. But she didn't lock either door when she left."

"Why not? Surely someone might have just walked in and found you?" asked Min.

"Maybe she wanted them to. Maybe she wanted me freed sooner rather than later. Maybe this is all about something else entirely. I honestly don't understand what is going on. Maybe she simply forgot to lock the doors."

"If you tie someone up and impersonate them, you don't want them to be found. This is getting weirder by the minute." I checked the door leading into the church but it was definitely locked. Why would they have been left open earlier? Unless the killer was meant to come and the key had been left somewhere. That must have been it. Or they wanted something from inside and the dead woman had given them the key. So much confusion.

"Is there a spare key to the doors?" I wondered.

"Yes, of course! Sorry, my brain's addled and I'm not thinking straight. We have a whole mess of keys in the drawer. I serve several churches, so have to keep all the keys, and it gets rather messy but they should be in here somewhere." Natasha opened a desk drawer and pulled out bunch after bunch of keys, muttering while she rifled through the drawer.

"That's a lot of keys," laughed Min.

"I know. I label them so I keep track, and this is my home church so where I store them, but I'm afraid I might not have been as organised with the spares. Each church has a minimum of three keys, if not a handful, so it's chaotic at times. Ah, here we go."

I took the keys she offered then unlocked both doors, checking outside before opening them wide. We headed back into the church, the sound of our slow footsteps eerily loud as we walked down the aisle in single file. Exiting and stepping into glorious sunshine was astonishingly beautiful, the well-maintained graveyard and small garden delightful.

Natasha smiled as she lifted her head to the sun and spoke softly without looking at us. "It's a beautiful place. The clipped yew, the flowers, the gravestones. It's so tranquil. Some people find graveyards spooky, but I've always found them a place of peace. Ideal for contemplation and a reminder that all is impermanent."

"You aren't your average vicar, are you?" I teased. "How old are you?"

"Forty-three, so quite young for the responsibility, but this is a quiet parish and my superiors felt it could do with a, as they put it, 'youngster' to attract a more youthful crowd. It's been going quite well, and we hold a lot of events at the churches to attract a new generation, but it's exhausting."

Min put an arm around Natasha and said, "It sounds like you're doing a great job. Did you grow up here?"

"Yes, in this town, actually. Craven Oaks is my home and unless I get sent away to look after another parish, I hope I remain here. I've worked all over the country, but I was promised this would be my permanent home now."

"What's it like living here?" I asked.

"Great. The people are friendly, there's no problem with newcomers not being welcome like in some towns, as it's always been a real mix of Welsh and English, with families coming and going over the years, so we have a nice combination. The shops are mostly independent, which gives it that timeless village feel, and we have a proper butchers, a deli, a fantastic cake shop, plus the usual Co-op, a petrol station, and just out of town you have the large supermarkets. It has everything you could ever need."

"Sounds idyllic," sighed Min, catching my eye.

I smiled, and agreed, "It does. A perfect place to make a new life."

"Absolutely." Natasha smiled, but then she swayed and almost collapsed so I grabbed her and guided her to a bench. "Thank you. I think that took rather more out of me than I'd realised."

"It's a lot to take in. You must have been so scared." Min sat beside her and held her hand.

"Strangely, no. I felt quite calm once the initial shock wore off. Whoever that woman was, she was clearly troubled. I don't think she wanted to hurt me. I got the impression she didn't want to be involved in this at all."

"What gives you that idea?"

"The way she acted. She kept apologising for tying me up. I did try to stop her, to fight back, but she was surprisingly strong. I need to go to the gym more often."

"Don't you find the time to go much?" asked Min.

Natasha giggled. "By going more, I meant going at all. But that woman, she seemed almost like she was being forced. Maybe I'm wrong and she was simply a polite kidnapper, but that's not the impression I got."

"It still doesn't help us figure out why she was doing it." I rubbed at my beard, trying to understand, but got nothing. "We're so sorry you were involved. By the sounds of it, it's our fault."

"No, don't say that. Maybe her plan was to disrupt your wedding. She certainly asked about the change of venue and mentioned you both by name, but you aren't to blame. You're a lovely couple, and don't deserve any of this. Maybe there is a simple explanation and this will make sense. My concern right now is for my parishioners. We still have a killer on the loose."

"We do. I better go and check nobody is close by. We don't want them seeing such an upsetting sight." I nodded to Min, then called Anxious, and we went to wait by the mystery woman until the police arrived.

We skirted the church, then hurried around the corner to the back and the large pine tree where she was pinned. Anxious stopped by a bench and yipped, so I followed him over. He was staring suspiciously at a small handmade mouse, crocheted by the looks of it, with tiny mouse babies on the figure's shoulders. Little plastic flowers were tied to the bench.

"That's cute. A memorial maybe?"

Anxious howled, then edged forward, still sitting, and sniffed the figures before turning to me and flattening his ears.

"Hey, it's probably a little way of remembering the dead," I suggested. "People like to leave flowers and things in the places those who passed spent time."

Anxious stood, turned his back on it, then with a huff raced off to the tree. I jogged after him, took one look at the corpse, then turned my back on her, which felt disrespectful, and waited for the authorities to arrive.

Chapter 6

Ambulance sirens were the first sign that the peace would soon be disrupted, followed soon after by the wail of police vehicles. Less than a minute later, we were swamped by paramedics, police officers, two detectives, a photographer, crime scene investigators, and other assorted teams. I joined Min and Natasha back at the entrance, and after a brief explanation to the detectives, we were left alone while they investigated.

Teams were directed to the tree whilst others went inside to look over the scene of the kidnapping; we could do nothing but wait.

Anxious grew bored very quickly, never one to stay put for long if he was awake, so he hopped up onto Natasha's lap and curled up with a groan, making sure we knew this was not how he'd planned to spend his Saturday. Neither had we.

The moment he settled, Natasha had to hand him over to Min as the paramedics wanted to check her over properly at the ambulance. Then she would have to give a proper statement before being allowed to go about her business if she was given the all-clear.

We said goodbye in case we didn't catch up later, but she promised to call to see what news there was. We thanked her again for being so gracious as it seemed like this was about us somehow, then sat and watched the teams go about their business.

As was always the case with murder scenes, there was an inordinate amount of coming and going, with groups of people talking things over, orders being given, tape being strung up like Halloween decorations, and a general atmosphere of barely contained chaos.

Two detectives named Karl and Monroe were old hands at this, having both worked in large cities before moving to the peaceful Shropshire countryside for a more relaxed way of life, keen to offer their backstory and their surprise at such a horrific murder—the first for many years in the area. Both in their fifties, they were relaxed, friendly, and keen to hear tales of my past involvement in similar cases as they knew who I was, and for a change didn't mind at all.

It was refreshing, and allowed us to relax while we went over the weird wedding interruption, the missing fake vicar, our trip into town, and finding first Natasha then the corpse. They listened, asked appropriate questions, and seemed satisfied with our story, if rather incredulous, which was understandable.

When we'd finished, they told us that we were free to leave, but that it would be best-advised if we stayed in the area. They'd be up at the campsite later to speak to everyone else, but it would be a quick visit as the scene of the crime was where their focus lay.

"Are we allowed to ask around? See what we can uncover?" I asked politely, dreading getting into an argument, hoping they would see our side of things.

"Can we stop you?" asked Karl with a smirk and a raised eyebrow on his tanned face.

"You could try," I said with a smile.

"Relax, Max," said Monroe. "We know about your exploits, and are happy for you to do your thing. There's no point trying to be discreet around here and hide what you're up to from us, as small towns like this mean everyone knows your business, but we're cool with you helping. All we want is for the killer to be found, and an explanation. If you can do that, we're all for it."

"But," Karl held up a hand, "don't forget that there is a killer on the loose who may still be after you. We don't know for sure that this is done with, and that's a real concern. Most likely, they're long gone, but who knows? This is a real head-scratcher, so until we have our killer you should keep a low profile and remain with your family. Safety in numbers and all that."

"Thanks. We'll be careful."

They nodded, then approached a team of officers by the church steps and were soon deep in conversation.

"They seemed nice," said Min. "Professional, polite, and different to some of the detectives we've dealt with."

I raised an eyebrow and said, "You're skirting over the one massive elephant in the room."

Min tittered, and covered her mouth with her hand, mischief flashing in her eyes. "Am I? And what could that be?"

"We have this image in our head of what detectives should look like. But c'mon, they weren't exactly dressed how you'd expect."

"I don't know what you mean." Min couldn't contain her mirth a moment longer and burst out laughing.

I chuckled as I said, "The magician's outfits. Why were they dressed as magicians?"

"Maybe they're going to a fancy-dress party."

"It's one o'clock in the afternoon."

Min bellowed, causing those in the vicinity to turn and stare. She covered her face with her hands, trying to contain herself, and gradually got things under control.

"Oh no!"

I turned to where she was looking and saw the two detectives heading our way. "Look what you've done now. They'll think you're making fun of them."

"I wasn't. I didn't mean to. It was just odd, that's all."

"We forgot to mention," said Karl, smiling, "that we're doing a little magic show in The King's Head pub later. In the beer garden. We should probably skip it because of the murder, but we promised. You're welcome to join us. Might be a way to relax."

"Um, that's very kind of you," I said. "So, er, you're magicians?"

Karl and Monroe exchanged a confused look, then Monroe asked, "Why did you think we were dressed like this?"

"We didn't want to pry. It's not our place to ask."

"That's weird, Max, if you don't mind me saying so."

"Yeah, Max, super weird," gasped Min, her cheeks flushed as she tried to hold in her laughter.

Monroe frowned, then said, "Anyway, you're welcome to attend. We do a regular spot, and also do kids' parties, fetes, any events really. It's a lot of fun."

"We'll try to make it. What time?"

"About four, although these things are usually very casual. Maybe see you later?" said Karl.

We nodded, then they left again.

"That was a close one. Do you think they noticed I was laughing?" Min nudged me painfully in the ribs, and added, "Wonder what tricks they do? It's a bit weird turning up to a crime scene wearing matching black magician outfits with coat tails and wands. Monroe even had a dove poking out of his suit jacket. And Karl had one of those never-ending handkerchiefs up his sleeve. He kept pulling it in and out and I don't even think he realised."

"It definitely wasn't the usual way you get introduced. They seem cool about it, though, and weren't embarrassed or anything. I guess everyone knows them and what they do."

"Maybe we should go?" Min batted her eyelashes and put a hand on my thigh.

"How can I resist? And it will be a good way to meet some locals and keep an eye on things. Maybe the killer will be there."

"You think? That would be cool." I tutted as I wagged a finger, and she stammered, "Maybe not cool, but intriguing. Is that a better word?"

"Much. Shall we go back to Vee and make a cuppa and have lunch? I'm starving. I know it feels wrong to be hungry after all this, but it's been a stressful morning."

"Too right it has. I was so nervous when we were getting married, and this morning my stomach was in knots."

"Yours too? I thought it was just me."

"Max, it's our big day. Or was. Even though we've been married before, it still made me nervous."

"Come on, let's go eat, then maybe we should pop in to the camping shop and see if they sold any paracord to a fake vicar lately."

"It's a date!" Min stood, then held out her hand. I took it and squeezed tight, my love overflowing for this beautiful, happy, kind woman I was lucky enough to be loved by.

With Anxious cradled in my arms, and the exhausted little fella fast asleep, we skirted the various teams and exited the churchyard then hurried back to Vee. My heart beat a little faster as I spied the orange and white classic campervan, unable to stop a smile spreading. I turned to Min to find her equally happy.

"Isn't she beautiful?" sighed Min. "I know it's silly, but it makes me happy just seeing her. She's special, isn't she?"

"Very. And even more special now we're going to be in her together. Think you can cope?"

"Of course I can. I adore her. And anyway, with the gazebo up it's like having a triple-sized home. All we need is to get Anxious to sleep up on the pop-top bed platform and then we'll actually have enough space to sleep comfortably."

I turned to Min, gobsmacked, and admitted, "I'd never thought of trying that. Think he'll go for it?"

We looked down at the snoring guy, his nose twitching, the brown patches on his white fur as familiar as my own hands.

"Are you kidding? As if! No way will he want to miss out on midnight cuddles and stealing our pillows. And besides, I like it."

"Me too. One big, squashed but happy family. How it should be."

"There you go then. But I'm not spending a winter without a diesel heater, so you need to figure out how to do it."

"I'm not going to do that myself. I don't want to risk killing us in our sleep."

"Max, you need to get a carbon monoxide doo-dah."

"We already have one. And a fire extinguisher. Plus those blankets for smothering fires."

"Then we're all set. And I've been watching YouTube videos about installing the heaters. It's easy. You just have to tap into the fuel tank, run a flexi pipe, and cut a hole in the floor and—"

"You've been watching videos about it? What else?"

"Loads of stuff. How to make fly curtains to stop the bugs, tips for optimising space, and even a few videos about what to do about the lack of a toilet, but I won't go into details about that."

"Then I'll leave the heater installation to you," I teased, winking. I opened up the side door, put Anxious on the bench seat, then made a coffee on the built-in hob, something I rarely used as cooking inside a vehicle never ended well. Grease over the windows and upholstery, the smells, and the cramped conditions made cooking in the gazebo much more preferable.

Although not exactly a prime location, we nevertheless enjoyed our coffee while Min sat on the floor of Vee and I used the little collapsible step as a stool. There's no denying the smugness factor of being able to make a brew wherever you fancy, even if it is in a car park. Maybe even more so, as it's like having your kitchen with you at all times, and despite the vast array of cafes, when you've had a stressful day a homemade cuppa always tastes better than anything you can buy.

We picked at our lunch, but once the initial hunger was sated neither of us had much appetite or enthusiasm but ate rather machine-like, knowing we needed sustenance but hardly tasting it as our minds were elsewhere. Anxious, on the other hand, was all stomach and gladly snaffled whatever remained.

With lunch done with, I locked up and we headed back into the town, not in the mood for sightseeing but nevertheless impressed with the variety of shops, the prices, and the quality of the produce we spied as we passed by the windows of shops with gleaming glass and smiling staff.

The camping shop was an independent. A narrow, long place that smelled of adventure and muddy boots. The moment we stepped inside I liked it; this was my kind of place. Tatty around the edges, but rammed full of gear, nothing like the large out-of-town chain businesses that always felt rather sterile even though they offered great prices in what seemed to be a permanent sale.

Craven Oaks Camping Oasis was nothing like that. It was for those who were serious about their equipment, as well as catering to the tourist crowd. Along with all manner of clothing from budget to eye-watering—who could bring themselves to spend three hundred pounds on a lightweight coat to shave a few ounces off the weight?—they stocked footwear ranging from Dunlop wellies to Le Chameau— well worth the terrifying cost—and more socks than seemed strictly necessary.

But it was the gear that mesmerised me. This wasn't just a camping and outdoors supplier, they had a whole massive section for the campervan community. Cheap diesel heaters, power banks ranging from pocket-sized right up to the large Bluettis and other brands that could see you comfortable for a week without a recharge if you were careful. The offerings continued with endless USB powered taps, tiny camping stoves, little fold-out tables, and cleverly designed storage solutions that left me drooling and wondering how much I was allowed to spend in a single day without the bank shutting down my card.

I had to get a grip on myself otherwise I'd go crazy, so just browsed, vowing to return at a later date for a second look rather than be impulsive. This was the real issue with vanlife, and camping in general. It was so easy to get carried away with shiny object syndrome and blow more cash than you could ever justify just because you liked the look of the latest collapsible fire bowl or the newest and smartest way to boil a kettle. And oh boy, did they have kettles! Gleaming miniature ones, old black beaten up ones perfect for hanging over an open fire, and even Le Crueset in traditional orange for that touch of class in the campervan.

"Come on, Max, step away from the kettles and cookware. You're dribbling all over the Lodge frying pans," teased Min, taking my arm and dragging me from the back of the store.

I spun and caught a final look at a set of Shun knives, then allowed her to guide me past the sleeping bag section —did we need new ones?—towards the man behind the till set halfway into the shop against a wall. Behind him, rows of gas canisters were lined up like keen soldiers, with more tiny gas burners, and the serving counter was a glass cabinet stocked with knives that I just had to have.

"I think I'm in heaven," I joked to the heavily bearded man as he glanced up.

"Then I've done my job well. Anything in particular take your fancy?"

"Just all the knives and kettles, and the easy install shelves, and I think I need a collapsible bucket and maybe a new washing-up bowl. Did I see one with a matching drainer?"

"You did!" he chuckled, stroking his beard as his eyes lit up with pound signs. "Let me guess. You're a vanlifer, most likely a VW owner, and not the new ones but a classic. You like to make meals outdoors to save the smells, are a keen cook, and own quality cookware. I bet you're organised and buy the best quality, and have been trying and trying to get every item smaller and only keep what you really need and are always looking for ways to improve on space and efficiency. Am I right?"

"Whoa! That was spooky," I said, grinning.

"Very astute," agreed Min. "You saw us in the car park, didn't you?" she accused.

The owner held his hands up and admitted, "I did. I was on my lunch break and was coming back when I saw you two looking smug drinking a coffee, and knew straight away you'd be in here."

"How did you know we'd be in here?" I wondered.

"Most vanlifers and enthusiasts come in. Everyone knows about the place. But that's not the reason. I heard about what happened at the church, and someone dropped your name, Max. I know all about you. Most keen van owners do. Pleasure to meet you. I'm Ken, but most people call me Swede."

"Nice to meet you, Swede." We shook hands then Min did likewise, and because he was already whining I lifted Anxious up and after he got a head rub I introduced him too. After the usual explanation regards his name, Anxious shook paws then I let him down.

"Are you actually Swedish?" asked Min. "I can hear a faint accent, but can't place it."

"It's Canadian. I lived there until I was ten, then we moved here. My Dad's Swedish, and although my accent is Canadian everyone thought I was from Sweden anyway so the nickname stuck. Now, can I assume you've come here because of the murder? Terrible business. Care to fill me in? All I heard was that some woman impersonated the vicar, tried to ruin your wedding, vanished halfway through, had tied up Natasha, and was murdered. Pinned to a tree with a poker."

"Then you know as much as us," I sighed. "I guess news really does travel fast around here."

"Faster than you can run down the high street," he chuckled. "So, are you on the case? I bet you are, what with it being your wedding that was ruined. You both seem made for each other though. Such a lovely couple. I love reading your wiki, and some of the comments on the forum are hilarious. Your dad does a good job of running everything."

"Um, thanks, I think. He shares too much personal stuff, though."

Swede grinned and said, "I'm guessing you don't read it, as you don't know the half of it."

I groaned, Anxious covered his eyes, and Min pinched my bum, so things were looking up. With a high-pitched yelp, and a cheesy grin for my favourite lady, I asked Swede, "Do you own this place?"

"Sure do. Dad's a hiking nut and opened the shop thirty years ago before walking was as popular as now. But his was the only place in the area and always did alright. I used to work after school and weekends and got the outdoors bug too. He retired a few years back, so I took over. Made a lot of changes he wasn't too happy about, as he's not one of those guys who likes everything lightweight and minimal, but when he saw the books he changed his mind, the wily old sod." Swede laughed, and smoothed his beard.

He was one of those guys who not only had a beard, but "a beard" in the fullest sense. No patchy bits for him. It was over his cheeks, right down his neck, and although not as long as mine, it was very full and made his round and puffy cheeks look like little balls trying to fight for their freedom. A rather portly guy, he was solid, and undeniably fit, but clearly indulged in hearty, calorie-dense meals whilst out in the elements.

Unlike most of the people in the shop, he wore a Black Sabbath faded tee and green camo shorts. His shock of salmon-red hair complemented his ruddy complexion, and he even had a decent tan, something rare for redheads.

"So, shoot!" Swede leaned forward, eyebrows dancing, and whispered, "You have questions, right? Is it to do with the murder?"

"If that's okay?" asked Min.

"Sure. Everyone likes Natasha, and we're all rooting for you guys, so ask away."

"I guess you already know what happened, so it's fine to share details," I began. "Natasha was tied up with paracord. About a centimetre thick, red and black, and a lot of it. The woman who was pinned to the tree was tied with the same stuff. Natasha said she had it in her bag. As far as we could tell, it was brand new. It had that smell to it, you know?"

"Sure, nothing like the smell of new paracord in the morning."

"Right, okay. Um, so do you sell it?"

"Course we do. We have a whole section for the serious climbers, and they use loads. Campers use it for all sorts, too, as it's really versatile. Let's go take a look." Swede came out from behind the counter then led us right to the rear of the shop where a section of wall was taken up with carabiners and climbing gear, with reels of cord and rope. There were more large bundles on the floor and in boxes, and I expected there was more stock out the back too.

"That looks like it," said Min as she pulled a pack from a hook.

"Yes, that's it."

"There you go then." Swede smiled, like we had our answer.

"But did you sell any to anyone recently?" I asked.

Swede frowned. "I'm not following."

"Maybe you sold it to the murderer, or the dead woman."

"Oh, right. Look, guys, I didn't think you actually wanted to know if I sold it to the killer. I sell tons of stuff every single day. I can't keep track of individual sales."

Min frowned and said, "That's a shame."

Swede suddenly burst out laughing, startling us, and Anxious howled, worried we were under attack. "I'm just messing with you guys. Chill out. You should have seen you faces. Yes, I remember selling a few bundles recently. In fact, I sold some yesterday to this guy. Said he was off on a hike and wanted to secure his backpack. And I think he wanted to replace a guy rope. I told him we sold those, too, but he said the paracord would be fine. Bit shifty, but nice enough. No idea who he was though."

"Anyone else?"

"A woman a few days before that. She bought this stuff too. One of the smaller packs though. Not enough to tie someone up with and have any spare. And, yeah, now I think about it, some woman did come in yesterday and was a bit suspicious. I can tell a dodgy character a mile off. She bought one of the large packs too. But there were also a few other sales, and I'm not sure what sizes everyone bought. I just ring up the till and process the cards."

"Thanks, Swede. It might help, and if we need to ask you any more questions is it okay to come back?"

"Sure, Max. Any time."

Chapter 7

Min dragged me out of vanlife and outdoors heaven and into the heat of the afternoon. I took a longing glance back at the shopfront, so innocuous from outside, not even hinting at the treasures it contained.

"You're still thinking about that kettle, aren't you?"

"And that clever compact coffee thingy. You can plunge it straight into a cup of hot water and get a perfect coffee. Did you see how tiny it was?"

"Yes, and you absolutely don't need it. Remember, we need a large pot every day now it's the two of us."

"If we ever manage to get married."

"Max, don't worry, everything will work out in the end. It's destiny. Our destiny."

"Wow, you're being very upbeat. Min, how are you taking this so well? Our big day is ruined. Rather than a wedding and a fun party, we've got a kidnapped vicar and a dead vicar impersonator. It's not exactly fortuitous."

"Maybe not, but it depends how you look at it. I've decided to look on the bright side of this. On the positive."

"Oh, and what are the positives?"

"We're staying at a great place with loads of character. We have the site to ourselves. Just us, family, and friends. And we met a lovely lady and saved her. Natasha seems nice, doesn't she?"

"She seems great. I'm amazed how well she handled everything. I bet she's a wreck though. Min, you're a real lifesaver, and I mean that literally. I don't know what I'd have done without you."

"Max, what are you talking about? You've been off on your own travelling around in Vee, and I've been so jealous and slightly in awe of how you handled the mad things that happened to you."

"Thanks, but I think sometimes I appear braver than I actually am."

"Nonsense! You keep a cool head, don't let the horrid things affect you too much, and still find the time to cook amazing meals, visit incredible places, and handle living in a confined space. It's admirable."

"It's all because of you. That's how I handle things. Knowing that one day you'd be with me and the little guy again."

"And now I am. Well, almost." Min winked, and it lifted my spirits no end.

"Come on, I guess we better get back to the site and let everyone know what's happening. Maybe they'll want to come to the pub later and we can watch the magic show, have a drink, and chat with some people. We might get a lead. Someone has to know something."

"I get the feeling that whoever did this hasn't finished yet." Min shuddered, and scooted over as if the sun had vanished behind thick cloud cover, but it was anything but cool, especially with her so close to me.

"What makes you say that? Who could be next?"

"Max, I have no idea, but nothing about this rings true. It makes no sense. Natasha seems to think that the woman who tied her up didn't really want to do it. Like she was being forced. Maybe that's true, maybe she was just nervous, or maybe that's what she wanted her to think, but either way she ended up dead. Someone else is behind this, obviously, and what on earth could their motive have been?"

"I'm struggling to come up with anything, to be honest," I admitted. "It's the strangest thing we've ever been involved in. What could anyone possibly gain by pretending to marry us? And why did the woman duck out halfway through and vanish like that?"

"Unless that was the point. To disrupt things and send us off on this crazy adventure."

"You mean it was planned that the wedding wouldn't be finished?"

"Maybe. Is it possible that the killer had everything worked out in advance? That they were up at the campsite the whole time, maybe even inside the static caravan, and the dead woman was told to go inside before the ceremony was completed?"

"And they'd planned on killing her back at the church? But why?"

"No idea! It's just a silly suggestion anyway. The truth is out there somewhere though."

"Then we better get busy trying to find it. But not too busy. I'm exhausted already, and it's only early afternoon. I don't think I can take any more surprises."

"Me either. But then, it wouldn't be our wedding day if something crazy didn't happen. I'm actually relieved it hasn't been something more shocking."

My mouth opened and closed, but the words failed me. Eventually, I blurted, "Something more shocking? Fake vicars? Real ones tied to chairs? Dead women impaled with pokers? You don't call that shocking?"

Min batted my arm and said, "Of course I do. What I mean is that I expected something would happen, and it could have been worse."

"I really don't know how, but okay, I'll go with it. Hey, we should check out the place that sells the pokers. We might learn something there. Maybe it's a disgruntled blacksmith, and this is about getting revenge on whoever the woman was."

"It's worth a try. At the very least, we might discover if someone bought the poker recently. They might have actually got it today."

We stopped a man striding along the high street like he had places to be, and he rather abruptly told us where the ironmonger's was. We followed his directions and turned off the main street then wandered past a series of charity shops, a bookstore, and a second-hand furniture shop doing a roaring trade judging by the number of people inside. At the end of the short road we stopped outside what I knew was like an Aladdin's cave to Min, and got me excited too.

"Here we go again," I sighed, grinning at her.

"You know I love these places, but don't go pretending that you don't!" Min eyed the stack of galvanised buckets and tier upon tier of plastic boxes with greedy eyes. I had to drag her past them, but got distracted by all the traditional brooms made from sticks and began thinking that maybe I really needed one and what a cheap price they were.

"Focus, Max," Min giggled, her eyes drawn to the shop window where all manner of ironmongery was on display.

"It's hard when they have so much cool stuff. Would it be in bad taste to buy a poker? I love how the metal is twisted, and the handle looks incredible. It's made from one piece just like the one that... er, um, no, on second thoughts I think I'll pass."

"They do look very nice, but maybe today isn't the best day to pick one up. Let's go in and see if they dealt with anyone dodgy." Before I could stop her, Min marched through the open door into the gloomy interior. With Anxious still fast asleep in my arms, and I wasn't quite sure why I was still carrying him as surely he couldn't be that tired, I followed in Min's excitable wake.

The ironmonger's was a traditional shop with a counter stretching the entire length of the side wall, behind which a series of ancient wooden drawers held mysteries only known to those who needed to know and the large pot-bellied man serving a customer. We waited until they'd finished, then stepped up to the counter.

Before we could even ask, the man smiled at us and introduced himself as Phil, owner, and the latest in a long line of blacksmiths who had run the business for generations going back to the seventeen hundreds. I got the feeling that Phil would have given us their names if we'd asked, or even if we didn't, but Min managed to ask about the pokers before he got too far into it and we went down the rabbit hole of local chitchat that he was clearly so fond of.

"A poker you say?" he mused, rubbing at his grey stubble, his eyes roaming.

"Yes, like the ones in the window."

Phil's eyes widened in mock horror. "Ah, this about the murder?"

"You know about it?" I wasn't surprised.

"Course I do. Happened ages ago now, didn't it? And the detectives just left. Hey, you going to catch the magic show later? Karl and Monroe always put on great entertainment. You should go."

"We might, yes," said Min. "What did they want to ask you?"

"Same as you pair," Phil shrugged. "And they warned me you two might put in an appearance. Said I was to help if I could, but not to encourage you too much." Phil chuckled, like there was a private joke we weren't privy to.

"That was kind of them." Min leaned forward, checked we weren't being overheard, which we were by every person in the shop, then asked, "And what did you tell the detectives?"

"Same as I'm about to tell you. That I make every single one of them pokers, and the other ironwork, and I sell about three a day. Mostly to the tourists, but a few locals too. I sold one this morning to Mary from down the road, and yesterday I sold five, but they were out-of-towners, couples out for day trips and what have you. Nothing suspicious about them, and I don't have any details or anything like that. Sorry, but it isn't much help. Bit mad my poker being used like that, but they're quality craftsmanship and are certainly up to the job of pinning someone to a tree. Not that I encourage that sort of behaviour," he added, frowning.

"Of course not. Thank you for your help, Phil. It's appreciated."

"Hey, no problem!" Phil turned as someone entered the shop, and called out, "Hi, Mary. Not come for another poker, have you?" He explained to us, "This is the woman that bought one this morning."

"Yes, and someone's nicked it! Can you believe that, Phil? They stole my poker. What's the world coming to when an old lady can't even leave her shopping outside her own front door and gets robbed!? They took my bags too. All my food."

"You forgot to take it inside again didn't you?" Phil tutted and shook his head in sympathy. "You should have got your lad to do it. He should help his mum."

"Might have got distracted when I went inside and made a cup of tea for us. But then I remembered about it and went to get my things and they were all gone. I had a nice bit of gammon for my tea, too, and that's vanished as well. Blooming thieves. Never used to be like this when I was a youngster. You could leave your front door open and never think twice about it."

"Mary's lived here her whole life," explained Phil. "Born in the house she lives in, never moved out, and knows everyone in these parts."

"And now I'm old and people are taking advantage. Who are you?" she snapped, looking me up and down, eyes lingering on my choice of footwear. She shook her mass of silver curls, then her eyes met mine and she hissed, "You aren't meant to wear Crocs in public. Everyone knows that."

"I'm a maverick," I laughed. "I'm Max, and this is Min. We're the ones who found the vicar."

"And the corpse," added Phil helpfully.

"I heard about you." Mary made it sound like an accusation, but I got the impression it was just her way.

"Really? What did you hear?" Min gave Mary her best smile, which seemed to soften her attitude immediately.

"That you were meant to be getting married up at Carl and Maureen's place. Lovely couple, they are. But someone tied up the vicar then pretended to be Natasha, then they got murdered. And with my poker, I bet! My poker! I already told the police, and they said I can't have it back. I don't see why not, as what use is it to them?"

"Now, Mary, you know they'll need that as evidence. It was used in a murder, so they can't hand it over to you."

"No, I'd expect them to wipe the blood off first," she giggled.

"Did you see anyone hanging around?" I asked.

"Nobody suspicious. But I keep to myself and don't like to make a fuss."

Phil stifled a laugh and turned away when Mary's head snapped around.

"We're sorry about your poker and the shopping," said Min. "That's awful. What was the poker for?"

Mary squinted at Min and looked up into her eyes. "Are you being funny? It's a poker for the fire. What do you think I was going to do with it?"

"I, er, meant, isn't it rather warm for having a fire?"

"Not when you get to my age, it isn't. I have a fire every day and I enjoy the routine. I cook on it, boil the kettle, and I like to lead a simple life."

"Mary doesn't even have a TV," said Phil now he'd recovered. "And here, Mary, this one is on me. Don't lose it." Phil retrieved a poker from behind the counter and laid it down.

"That's so sweet, Phil. Thank you so much. Now, I must be going. Things to do, people to see. Nice meeting you both." Mary smiled and nodded, then went to leave.

"Don't forget your poker," Phil reminded her.

With a chuckle, and a shake of her head, Mary grabbed the poker, her grip firm, and hefted it like it weighed nothing, her strength at odds with her slight frame, almost knocking Min out as she swung it, then wandered off.

"Do you really think someone stole her things?" I asked Phil once Mary had left.

"Doubtful. Mary's absent-minded, and most likely either left her shopping somewhere or she unpacked it and doesn't even remember."

"But it seems like they did use her poker," said Min.

"Maybe, or maybe not. It might have been one I sold to someone else. Mary's had three pokers and six buckets already this year. She swears blind they got stolen, but she's forgetful and can never find anything. Her house is right on the street, and quite narrow, but those old properties are deceptively spacious inside and she has this massive back garden. Keeps chickens, has a large vegetable plot, and is always pottering around. She puts something down then forgets and can't find it." Phil shrugged; he was clearly used to her ways. "Mind you, I bet you've noticed the decorations on some benches, and the crochet work she puts on top of the mail boxes. That's all her. She likes to leave little shrines and whatnot about the place. It helps her to remember folks we've lost. It's an ageing population, so we get more funerals than any of us would like."

"That was very kind of you giving her a new poker," I said. "And yes, we've noticed the little artworks and the memorials. That's so sweet of her."

"We look after each other around here. It's a close community, and characters like Mary are an asset. And besides, I'd never hear the end of it if I didn't sort her out."

"Thanks for all your help," I said. "So far, we're loving it here."

"Really? I'd have thought you'd be itching to leave. It hasn't been the welcome I'd have liked for you both. Doesn't give the place a good name at all having people attack vicars. Mind you, I bet I sell a load of pokers once the news of the murder gets around. Tourists love stuff like this."

"You really think people will want to buy one because of what happened?" asked Min.

"You bet!"

As if to prove his point, a couple wearing matching lightweight anoraks entered and asked if this was the place that sold the pokers used in the murder. With a wink, and practically rubbing his hands together, Phil began his spiel. We left him to it and exited the cool interior and hurried away from the buckets and stackable containers before we blew more money than we had sense.

"Maybe the old lady did it," said Min with a laugh. "Maybe she thought the mystery woman stole her poker, or maybe she did, and she lost the plot."

"Could be," I teased. "Or maybe it was Phil so he could sell more of them. Come to think of it, it might even have been Swede. Who knows what goes on around here?"

"Max, I was only teasing. But I guess stranger things have happened. For all we know, it was Carl and Maureen and that's why they're leaving in such a hurry. Doesn't it seem odd to you that they've left us to use the campsite without even being there?"

"A little, but they hadn't planned on anyone staying, so I guess they don't want to change their plans. To be fair, they aren't even running it as a campsite now."

"I know, but it's still strange. You're right, though, I'm definitely overthinking things. Imagine suspecting a forgetful old lady!" Min squeezed my hand, rather awkward because of Anxious, and we both looked down at him.

"I've been holding him for so long, I'd forgotten he was there. Think he's okay? He's never this sleepy, and certainly never this quiet."

"He's worn out by the excitement. With us together, it's tiring him out."

Anxious opened an eye and slowly a smile spread on his face. Either that, or he farted. As we laughed, and I accused him of pretending, I almost gagged as I got a whiff of something noxious.

"Time for you to get down," I said hurriedly, lowering him and shaking my arms about to get rid of the smell.

Anxious sat, eyes full of innocence as he stared up at us.

"Nobody is falling for that look," tittered Min, taking a step away. "Hey, I know her. Max," Min tugged at my arm and pulled me in tight, "it's that woman! There!" Min pointed at a lady of about our age standing outside a clothes shop. She was looking right at us, scowling harshly.

"Who is she? Why is she giving you the daggers? Blimey, if looks could kill you'd be deader than a fake vicar."

"She's that woman I told you about. The one who was on my books for a few years. Remember how badly it ended?"

"That's her? Well, you did a good job as she's so slim. I thought she was massive?"

"She was, but she stuck to my diet plan and I saw her every month. It was going so well until she started trying to bully me. Remember?"

"Of course I do. You were so upset. What's she doing here?"

"That's what I'd like to know."

Min and I exchanged a look, both thinking the same thing.

Chapter 8

"I'm going to go and have a word." Min bunched her hands, a wicked scowl on her face; it didn't suit her at all.

"Min, is that a good idea? I never see you like this. She really got to you, didn't she?"

"It was the worst. I've never had a client like her before. Sure, sometimes it doesn't work out, but it's usually amicable. People can get upset if they don't see instant results, and now and then they get angry and shout, or burst into tears, but Hayley was different. She's a bully."

"So why not leave it be? There's nothing to be gained by talking to her."

"Max, it might be her. She told me I hadn't seen the last of her, and that she'd get her revenge. She might be the killer."

"Get revenge for what? All you did was help her to lose weight, right?"

"Yes, but she didn't see it like that. When I explained to her that she needed to ease up on the dieting and take it slowly or she could make herself unwell, she lost the plot with me. She threatened to hit me, to get revenge when I told her it was best we parted ways as I couldn't be held responsible for her getting ill. She wouldn't listen to my advice, even after all I'd done for her."

"So let her be. Don't upset yourself."

"I have to talk to her. To be sure it wasn't Hayley. Maybe she made the dead woman do what she did. Max, we might have found our killer."

"She wouldn't do all that just to ruin the wedding, surely?"

"Somebody did, and I wouldn't put it past her. She's bad news through and through." Before I could stop her, Min glanced quickly to check the road was clear, then marched across, her back ramrod straight, her hands thankfully no longer bunched into fists, but I knew I wouldn't want to mess with her.

Hayley, who had been watching us the whole time, looked away and began to walk off, clearly not wanting a confrontation now she'd been spotted. Min called out her name and she paused, before pretending not to hear and hurrying up. Min shouted her name again, and this time Hayley stopped, then spun on a pair of pink shoes with thick soles that matched her denim shorts and complemented a green vest. Her bright red hair, which looked natural, stood out against the strong colours, and she had a decent tan. There was no doubt that Min's dietary advice had worked, but if anything Hayley was a little too thin, and I understood Min's reasoning behind no longer wanting her as a client. There was always a fine line to tread when helping people with their diets, as the last thing she wanted was for it to become an obsession and for people to win one battle only to lose another.

With Anxious by my side, the foul gases having finally dissipated, and him not looking in the least bit guilty, we checked the road then he walked to heel and we hurried to catch up with Min just as she reached Hayley.

"Are you following me, Hayley?" demanded Min.

Hayley glanced left, then right, then at me, eyes averted from Min.

"I'm Max."

"Hayley. Min, what are you doing here? I didn't know you knew this area." Hayley looked as guilty as Anxious in a deli, sausage roll in his mouth, but continued as though not wanting an answer. "It's lovely, and such a nice day too. Anyway, be seeing you."

"You wait right there. I want some answers. Why were you staring at us? Why didn't you stop when I called your name? And what are you doing here?"

"I love it here, so come every year or two if I have the time. The last few years have been too difficult because of my weight, but now I'm slim again I'm making the most of things."

"You aren't answering my question. After what you said to me, the threats you made, and now I see you following me. Were you spying on us?"

"Why would I do that?" hissed Hayley, snarling, and craning her neck until her face was dangerously close to Min's. "I don't care about you or that it's your wedding day. How did it go?" she asked, trying to look innocent, but a sly smile spreading across her flushed face.

"How did you know it was my wedding day? You've been following us, haven't you? What's this about?"

"It's not about anything. A friend told me, that's all, but I didn't know you were getting married here. Or not getting married, more like." Hayley laughed, mean and spiteful, and I worried Min would either punch her or tackle her to the ground, but she kept her cool, which was admirable.

"Hayley, I'm trying to be civil, but you're acting mean, almost cruel. You clearly know there was a problem, so how do you know that?"

"Because Max's dad posted about it on the forum."

"And why would you be reading that? Why are you following what we do online?"

Hayley shrugged, then admitted, "Just interested. I heard all about what Max has been up to lately, and then that you were getting back together. Good luck with that," she laughed, the sound forced. "You're both a walking disaster, always getting involved in other people's business. You deserve each other." Without another word or a goodbye nod, she turned and stomped off.

"I do not like that woman." Min turned to me, her anger gone, and brushed at her eyes. "I will not let her make me cry. Max, could it be her?"

"I don't think so. I don't like the fact she's here though. It's either one crazy coincidence, or she's been following you. Came on purpose, possibly to try and ruin things, but maybe she decided not to bother as the wedding didn't happen?"

"Or maybe she's up to something and hates that I spotted her."

"She might not be a very nice person, but do you really think she's a killer? It's an extreme way to get back at you for calling it quits with her as a client."

"Max, you didn't see how she acted when we last spoke. I've seen people upset or angry before, but nothing like her. There was something very unsettling about it, and I couldn't stop thinking about it for ages. But you're right, killing is another thing entirely."

"What do you think, Anxious?"

He turned and stared at us, then yipped once before lying down.

"What's got into him?" asked Min. "He pretended to be asleep for ages so you'd carry him, and he didn't even seem interested in Hayley. Maybe that means it wasn't her."

"I think I know what it is. He's upset because the ceremony didn't go ahead. Is that it?" I asked him as I bent and rubbed his head.

My best buddy licked my other hand, tail wagging, seemingly over the upset.

"I think you might be right, and he's just worn out after all the excitement. But I'm not sure he understood the wedding anyway. I know why he's pining. He wants to get back to the others. He loves your folks, and adores Ernie, and most likely wants to run around and play. Anxious, do you miss Jack, Jill, and Uncle Ernie?"

Like a shot, the little guy was on his feet, tail rotating like a jet engine, eyes wide, ears sharp.

I chuckled and admitted, "You're right. Come on, let's get back and explain what's been going on, then maybe we can gather the troops and come down to the pub in an hour or two."

"Great idea!"

Hand in hand, with Anxious now trotting along merrily, we returned to Vee then I drove us back to the campsite.

As we approached, I slowed, then pulled to a stop as a large Luton rental van was blocking the gate. I pulled into the parking spot on the left and we got out to stretch our legs rather than just sit waiting.

"I guess they really are leaving today," said Min.

"Looks that way. Think we should offer to help load the van? I wonder how much stuff they're taking."

"Maureen said that most of it had already been either sold or given away and they were leaving everything else, apart from a few things. They said their son was getting the rest, didn't they?"

"Yes, so why the large van?"

"Maybe they had more stuff than they realised. Let's go see."

"Min, stop being so nosy," I teased.

"You know I love seeing how people pack their vans. It's always been fun. I like the challenge of seeing how much you can get into them by arranging things properly."

"You know that's weird, don't you? You give me grief about being obsessive in the kitchen, yet your favourite thing is packing up a van with furniture?"

"I always used to offer to help friends when they hired vans. And remember when we moved into the house? I had it loaded to perfection. You couldn't have fitted another thing inside."

With my best serious face in place, I said, "You made us very proud of you."

"Hey, stop teasing." Min smiled, then jogged off ahead with Anxious by her side, keen to see what this latest game might be.

I trailed behind, keeping my eyes peeled just in case of I didn't know what.

Min was already chatting to Carl and Maureen at the back of the van, all three laughing at something.

"Hey," I said, with a wave and a smile.

"Max, look how well their son has loaded the Luton. What a work of art."

I looked inside, marvelling at the amount of furniture, boxes, bags, and assorted items, including more outdoor furniture than inside, along with a massive pile of random lengths of wood and thick planks. "Very nicely done, but it looks like you've been emptying barns not the house."

"Most of the indoor stuff has already gone ahead," said Carl, "but I enjoy my carpentry and some of the wood is really expensive so I want to take it. I have a nice new workshop ready and waiting for me, and I can't wait. I even bought a new lathe."

"Which cost nearly as much as the house," said Maureen with a tut and a smile full of love directed at her husband.

"Then enjoy your new home," I said. "We hope you'll be very happy there. Are you off now?"

"We are. One last look around the old place, then we have to leave. We're so sad to say goodbye, but looking forward to a new adventure, too, and being closer to family. Ah, here's Frankie now." Carl smiled as their son approached with a large box which he expertly stuffed into the last remaining spot, while also saying hello to us.

Carl made the introductions, and Frankie shook our hands, patted Anxious, who wasn't interested in saying hello and wandered off like he had more important things to do, leaving us to chat. Unlike his parents, he was a tall man, almost six five, with a solid frame and the largest hands I had ever seen. He was fit, tanned, and yet something felt off about him the minute we shook. His grip was weak, surprisingly so, even though his hand engulfed mine and made Min's look like a child's.

"I bet you have a lot of memories of this place," I said once we'd shaken.

"Oh boy, do I!" He smiled at his parents, then put an arm around each of them. "This pair kept me on my toes. Always work to be done, chores to do, but Mum always made sure I had a lovely dinner and I think that's why I never seemed to stop growing."

"His stomach was always like a bottomless pit," laughed Maureen, pride in her eyes.

"A really good boy," said Carl.

"Boy? I'm approaching fifty. Time for me to retire soon."

"You wouldn't know what to do with yourself," tutted Maureen. "You've always been a hard worker."

"True. I like to keep busy." Frankie cast a wistful look around the site, then snapped back to focus on us and with a laugh said, "I'll really miss this place. Are you both sure about this?"

"We're sure," said Carl. "We know you've been wanting us closer for years, and it's finally time to admit that we can't run the campsite any more. The gardens are too much work, let alone the rest of it, and we want a quiet life now. To be near you and the grandchildren."

"It'll be great to have you so close. I can pop in for a cuppa whenever I want."

"You didn't fancy running this place?" I asked.

They exchanged a look, but it was brief and easy to miss.

Frankie coughed politely and grunted, "Not my thing."

"Frankie prefers to have a more varied job, where he goes to different places every day. That's why he does the removals."

"But you don't have your own removal van?" I wondered.

"We have a few, but they're on jobs today. Quite often we end up using rentals as there are less overheads and it works out cheaper in the long run. The only issue is getting them when you need them, so we maintain a small fleet. Keeps me out of trouble though. Right, are we good to go?" he asked his parents.

Both nodded, but it was clear this was an emotional time.

"We'll leave you to say goodbye to the place," I said. "Thank you for letting us stay on for a while. Um, did you hear about what happened at the church?" I was surprised nobody had mentioned it, but they were clearly feeling very emotional and had their own things to deal with.

"Awful business," said Carl.

"The worst. At least Natasha is safe now. Frankie, you must have just missed all the trouble in town. You were there earlier, weren't you?"

"At the shops, yes, but I didn't see anything at all. First I heard was when one of your nosy neighbours called to tell you."

"They aren't nosy. They're looking out for us. Warning us of the trouble," said Maureen.

"If you say so, Mum." Frankie stepped up onto the rear of the van then pulled down the roller door, clearly keen to get on with the trip to Barnstaple.

Min and I tried not to look too intrigued by the news that Frankie had been in town earlier, and said goodbye then left Frankie to move the van so we could gain access. Just before we got into Vee, Carl came rushing over, meaning he hobbled on his stick, his dodgy hip clearly giving him trouble, and called out, "Don't forget, the offer still stands. Call if you want to buy the old place. It goes on the market the day after tomorrow, but if you get in first you can grab a real bargain. We just want this to be over with now." Carl was close to tears, so we thanked him, then hurried into Vee before he made himself more upset.

Frankie pulled the van over on the opposite side of the track, so I drove through the open gate and we waved at

Carl and Maureen. They didn't see us as they stood arm in arm and stared at the house.

"It must be so hard to leave somewhere you love so much. They clearly adore it here, but I suppose family comes first."

"It's what they want. They deserve to take it easy now. And by the sounds of it, they can't wait to spend more time with their grandkids." I pulled over before we got around the hedgerows to our hidden spot, keen to discuss this before we joined the others. "What did you make of Frankie?"

"His hands were way too soft to be a removal man, weren't they? Surely they'd be tougher from moving stuff all day?"

"That's what I thought. Maybe he's more like the boss than a worker."

"Could be." Min chewed at her bottom lip, then asked, "Was it just me, or do you think he was bitter about them selling up?"

"I got the same impression. Maybe he did want to have the place. Maybe he wanted to run the campsite."

"Or have the cash from the sale. But who knows, maybe his parents will share out the money. They've already bought their new bungalow, so they must have had large savings."

"They've probably saved their whole lives. I guess that isn't our business. I did get a weird vibe off Frankie though."

"Like he was hiding something. And he was in town this morning. He could have done it."

"And so could almost everyone else we met. The guy at the camping shop, or even Phil the blacksmith."

"And let's not forget Mary, the forgetful woman from the ironmonger's," laughed Min. "She's my choice so far."

"Then we better watch out, or she'll be after us with her new poker." I smiled, but then felt bad for making light of such a terrible thing, and admitted, "That was wrong. But boy do we have a lot of suspects already. What we really need is some kind of motive. And, no, I don't think it was Hayley just to get back at you."

"Neither do I now I've had a chance to think about it. That woman winds me up the wrong way. Come on, let's go tell everyone the bad news. I hope it won't put too much of a downer on the day."

"Are you kidding? Mum and Dad will be keen as anything to get involved now. You just wait and see."

And boy was I right!

Chapter 9

"Where have you been?" screeched Mum as she smashed her way past Dad and Uncle Ernie like a battering ram, sending them, their drinks, and their dignity flying.

"In town. We told you we were going. Is everything alright here?"

Before Mum had the chance to answer, Anxious yipped, then raced towards her and launched.

Mum's face went from a frown, to a smile, to one of utter, unbridled fear as she glanced down at her dress then up at the fast-approaching pooch, his tongue out, ears flapping, tail propelling him towards her at a speed impossible to dodge.

Dad, bless his heart, recovered from his assault, leapt to his feet, then flung himself sideways and intercepted Anxious then landed with him cradled in his arms, the crisis averted.

Anxious whined and licked, radiating happiness, then jumped off Dad once he was suitably soaked and ran over to Mum who had the sense to duck down and reach out before he jumped at her and got her dress dirty.

"Did you miss me?" she laughed, eyes bright with happiness and pride as she nodded to Dad then said, "My hero."

"Anything for my lady. Don't want your frock getting messed up."

Uncle Ernie hauled Dad to his feet, helped brush him down, then everyone gathered around and took turns giving Anxious plenty of attention until he lay down, back to normal now he'd got the gang back together.

"So, where have you been?" demanded Mum, linking her arm through Dad's and pulling him in close.

"We went to check on the real vicar and found her tied to a chair. Didn't Carl and Maureen come and tell you the news?"

"We haven't seen them," said Uncle Ernie. "Haven't seen a soul. Weren't people meant to be coming for the party?"

"Not until later. We said about six, I think. It's just us until then," I said. "So you don't know anything about what happened today?"

"You better tell us," said Dad.

"We found the vicar tied up, then someone locked us in the vestry, and by the time we got out it was too late and the woman who impersonated Natasha was dead. Pinned to a tree with a poker."

"Was it a nice one?" asked Mum.

"Um, yes, lovely. We went to the shop that sells them and had a chat with the owner, a bloke called Phil, then met this old lady who'd lost her poker, and before that we—"

"You better start at the beginning, Max," said Dad, nodding his head towards Mum who seemed to be holding her breath and seeing how red she could make her face.

"Oh, sorry, Mum. I know you hate it if you don't get the full story," I sighed, wishing I could chill out and have a glass of wine, rather than have to recount every minute of our day.

Mum gasped for air, her colour returning to normal, then smiled at me and gushed, "You're such a good boy. You know I like to be able to picture it in my mind. So, let's start again. You left here, then what happened?"

"We drove down into town, parked in the car park, then wandered over to the church and…"

It took a while, but we were allowed to pause the story to make ourselves comfortable and get a drink, before giving everyone the details. It was always like this, with my folks interrupting constantly, but Min was as patient as me, as she knew there was zero point in trying to resist my parents' insistence on getting the full picture, right down to what colour and style of clothes everyone was wearing and what the shops smelled like.

"Iron and horses," I said, in reply to the question about the ironmonger's smell.

"Why horses?" asked Uncle Ernie.

"I think they get a lot of horsey types coming in for supplies. They have a big shed out the back where people can pick stuff up, and it's one of those shops that caters to all sorts."

"Sounds fun," said Mum dreamily, eyeing her empty glass suspiciously then frowning at Dad like he was the one who had gulped her wine.

Dad topped her up without comment. She smiled at him; no words needed to be spoken. Min and I were worn out from not only the incredibly long day, but the sheer volume of people we'd had to deal with and the tale we'd just told, so with a lull in conversation we escaped to Vee for some peace just as Mum announced that she'd go and get ready for our trip into town. Nobody bothered arguing about it; going out meant a change of clothes and nothing would sway her from her polka dot path.

Anxious tagged along gratefully, and hopped onto the bench seat the moment we got inside. He curled up with a groan of pleasure, leaving us with hardly any space despite his diminutive stature. For such a small guy, he could really stretch out those little legs of his.

I sat on the step, while Min scooted Anxious over so she could perch on the bench, and we sipped our wine whilst the peace washed over us. Mum retreated into the large canvas bell tent we'd erected for her and Dad yesterday, an eight-person design but still too small for them because Mum didn't believe in travelling light. We'd made it really nice, though, with a cot bed, a sideboard, and even a little table, and added a few rugs the hire company supplied so it was like a home away from home. She hadn't even complained too much; a sure sign we'd done a fantastic job.

I glanced at Min, who was lost to her thoughts, a faraway look in her eyes, a gentle smile teasing the corners of her luscious lips, so I didn't interrupt. Instead, I let myself relax and actually take a moment to properly study the site without any interruptions, of which there had been countless since we arrived.

Tucked away down here out of sight of the main open field, I could still get a real feel for what the campsite was like and how it would be when full of guests. There were several such private areas, then the large field, all of which were surrounded by clearly previously well-maintained hedgerows allowed to grow rather tall to offer a sanctuary for birds and other wildlife. Behind that were little pockets of forest, with steep banks climbing up a hill on one side, the other leading towards the house then down the road towards the town.

If I listened really carefully, I could hear the gurgle of the stream as it tumbled over mossy rocks, deep in shade and incredibly cool, a true place of peace. It would be a delight at the height of summer when you wanted to cool off.

I pictured a swing hung from a large oak sat atop a low rise between the hidden pitches, maybe barbecue or campfire areas, picnic benches dotted about, and a new shower and toilet block. Nothing complex, just a simple operation, and definitely no electric hookup. Maybe even composting toilets. They were more popular than ever now.

Daydreaming like this, I realised I was getting rather into the idea, especially if we went down the glamping route and added a few bell tents like the ones we'd rented, because then we could stay in them and still be part of nature.

"Beautiful, isn't it?" Min squeezed beside me and sat, then took my hand.

"It really is. With a little work, this place could be absolutely incredible. Nothing complicated, but with some changes and some hard graft I could see myself staying here for months at a time. Even running it."

"Really? No more travelling?"

"I think vanlife will always be part of me now, but parking up at a site like this would mean it still felt like living in the van. There could be a laundry area and hot, free showers and some basic facilities."

"What about the house? You wouldn't want to live in it?"

"Maybe. I'm not sure. It could be rented out for holidays. It would earn a fortune and probably enough to cover running the entire site. Buying this place would take up a lot of money, and the repairs will most likely double the cost, especially because of the house and barns that need so much work, not to mention new water pipes and all the rest, but yes, I could live here. What about you?"

"I'd be happy wherever you were. I wouldn't want you to do anything just to please me then be miserable."

"Min, I've stayed at some sites for months, so living here wouldn't be that different. And trips can be taken whenever we feel like it."

"I could certainly make this my home. It's the prettiest, most magical place I've ever been to. It's brimming with potential and would be an amazing project to do while we're still young enough and have enough energy to do it."

"So, what are we saying?" I asked, knowing I was smiling.

"That we need to give it some serious thought, but that maybe it isn't the best idea. You're a vanlifer, a roamer, and might hate staying in one place."

"Like you said, I'd be happy living wherever you are."

Min kissed my cheek, then bounced to her feet and declared, "We need to get married. Nothing will stop us, will it?"

"Of course not. We'll make it official no matter what. Maybe we should get in touch with Natasha and see what she thinks. We can stay here until she's available."

"That's a wonderful idea. I hope she won't mind. She's been through an awful lot and might tell us to find someone else."

"We saved her. I'm sure she'll be fine about it. We might bump into her at the pub later. We can ask."

"Yes, let's do that!"

"Shall we see if the others are ready?"

Min laughed in sympathy, then said the obvious. "I'm sure Jill will let everyone know when it's time to leave. Max, should we go out? We have the party this evening and I'm not even sure if it should go ahead. But if it does, we need to prepare things. And don't forget about the huge paella. How long does that take to cook?"

"About half an hour's prep and the same to cook. Maybe less if everyone pitches in. We should be fine to nip out for an hour or so, as we told everyone to come at six. A few might be early, but they know the new location, so we'll be fine. It's going to be a great evening, Min, so don't worry about a thing, okay?"

"Okay. It seems weird to be having a party with nothing to celebrate."

"We're celebrating being alive. Being with friends and family and that we love each other. We might not be married legally, but as far as I'm concerned, you're already my wife. In fact, you always have been, no matter what the pieces of paper say."

"That's so sweet. Did you feel that way even when we were divorced? You weren't tempted to, you know, see someone else?"

"Never. I know it sounds silly, but even though we were divorced it felt more like we were separated but that if

I did what I should have years ago, things would work out. Maybe it was wishful thinking, but I did all I could to change. It took a lot of soul-searching until I made the move to quit work and leave everything behind but you. And how long did you last once I left properly and sold up and took off in Vee?"

"A day!" Min laughed, flinging her arms around me.

"Right? So maybe you felt the same way too?"

"Of course I did. Are you mad? You think I'd chase after you otherwise? Keep spending any free time I had with you guys? Max, this is all I ever wanted."

"I'm sorry I put you through so much. Truly. I feel so bad about it and have for years, even when I knew I was being neglectful and an idiot."

"No more talk about it. Ever. It's done. We've both learned valuable lessons that I don't think we'll ever forget, so let's leave it at that. If it helps, I forgive you. As long as you forgive me too."

"I do. Absolutely."

"Then it's settled. That part of our life is done for good. Like a bad dream. In fact, ever since we separated it's felt like a dream. Now it feels like I'm back to being myself, and that's because I'm part of you and you're part of me."

"And the little guy, of course," I teased, hugging her tight.

"Who could forget the bed thief? How is it that one tiny dog can be such a big presence?"

"He's a charmer alright."

"Cooee! Are you decent?" Mum ducked into the gazebo, resplendent in an indigo, wide-hemmed skirt with all the frills. Sleeveless as always, with just straps holding it up, revealing way too much chest for any son's liking, the white polka-dots brighter than the sun. The shoes were indigo to match, same as the bandanna, with her shock of always bright red dyed hair making her pale skin appear youthful as always beneath the heavy make-up. Mum frowned, and even tutted, shaking her head from side to side.

"What's wrong?" I asked. "And you look lovely, Mum. Very glamorous. Going somewhere nice?"

"Silly boy," she laughed, twirling. Then her brow creased and she pointed a finger at us. "Haven't you got ready yet?" Mum held up a hand. "What a daft question!" she giggled. "Of course you haven't. Come on, hurry up, we haven't got all day."

"Mum, we weren't planning on changing."

"But we're going out." Mum fidgeted; it clearly did not compute.

"We've already been out. I'm keeping my wedding clothes on, and so is Min."

"Min looks lovely as always, although white Crocs are still abhorrent. But what about your top and shorts, Min? And, Max, you just look like you're going to loaf about. Make the effort. A max effort." She doubled up laughing, and I vowed never, ever to forgive them for the name they gave me. Never!

"I'm fine as I am, Jill."

"Me too. It's the pub, to watch magic, and chat to whoever we can. This is what we were going to get married in, so if it's good enough for that, it's good enough for this."

"Suit yourself, but make sure you walk a few paces behind me so nobody knows we're together."

"Sure, Mum, we'll do just that." I nudged Min, whilst somehow managing to keep a straight face.

"I'll even walk backwards so it looks like I'm going in the opposite direction."

"Min Effort, are you being cheeky to your adorable mother-in-law?" demanded Mum, hands on hips, laser eyes firing up ready to do their worst.

"I… it… now don't go…"

"I'm only joking. How could I be mad at the best thing that ever happened to our Max? You're an angel, that's what you are."

"Thank you, Jill, and sorry for teasing. I look nice, though, don't I?"

"Of course you do. I was only teasing too. You both have your own styles and that's admirable. Did you know that some people think me and Jack dress a little over-the-top? Can you imagine?" Mum winked, then turned on her very high heels and left.

"She's such a sweetheart," said Min, standing and brushing her hands over her vest then frowning down at her Crocs. "Do you mind if I change them?"

"Of course not. I'll get my trainers on so you don't feel overdressed."

"Then hurry up. We wouldn't want to miss the magic show."

"Now this I am looking forward to." I couldn't imagine what we were letting ourselves in for, but something told me it would be a show never to be forgotten.

By the time we'd roused Anxious, then checked on a few things, everyone else was waiting. We'd all go in Vee, so Min squeezed into the back with Mum, Dad, and Anxious, while Uncle Ernie rode up front with me.

Ten minutes of Mum and Dad belting out a few Elvis classics meant I didn't manage to get a chat with Uncle Ernie, but I was sure we'd have plenty of time to catch up later on. Every so often I glanced in the rear-view to find Min grimacing, but trying to keep a smile plastered on her face as Mum and Dad sang at each other, with her in the middle.

It was obvious why my uncle wanted to ride shotgun, and I doubted he'd get the same luxury on the return journey. Min didn't mind a bit of Elvis, but only if it was sung by the King, not two fifties nuts with voices more suited to a silent disco. At least then everyone wore headphones, so could sing along to the real version rather than them murdering the song in more ways than you'd imagine possible.

We got there eventually, and it couldn't be a minute too soon.

Chapter 10

Set on the outskirts of town, The King's Head was a sprawling confusion of interconnected buildings, the oldest of which dated back to the fourteen hundreds. Over the centuries, additions had been made, from tiny extensions to a huge Edwardian building to the right of the squat original structure. Somehow, everything blended together to form a riot of architectural interest on the Grade II listed building as a whole. With thick stone roof tiles on parts, and slate on the rest, the fancy lead work, towering spiral chimneys in brick built to show off the wealth of a former landowner, and chunky carved window sills on some truly ancient parts, apparently taken from a monastery destroyed by fire over four hundred years ago, the place was intriguing, rather daunting, yet undeniably beautiful.

According to the information board sitting proudly beside the ancient oak and iron door that led into the original Ale House, many of the buildings were constructed from salvaged stone and brick. It included some clearly over-the-top features built into the once rather modest-sized building and larger later additions, making it a must-see for those interested in local history or ancient architecture.

With a large car park to the side, the pub itself sat proudly in a generous expanse of grass with a sloped bank leading down to a stream where wild flowers, nettles, and brambles vied for supremacy. Dotted around the manicured site were numerous picnic benches, and as we wandered around to take a look before going and ordering drinks, it came as a surprise how large the beer garden was. It wrapped right around the back where outbuildings of stone sat squat amongst more wild areas. Behind it all were fields of crops and tiny sections of ploughed land, and in the distance the Shropshire Hills wound their way in meandering curves, making me think of fluffy pillows and comfy beds.

A bright blue sky with nothing more than a few wispy clouds let the sun dazzle us and the beautiful countryside, and I honestly couldn't think of a more delightful place to be. It truly was a stunning part of the world, and one of the best beer gardens I'd ever visited. Rather than a mean patch of grass with beer barrels and old parasols stacked in a corner, the owners had put in considerable effort to make this a place worth visiting regardless of whether you wanted a pint or a coffee in a fantastic location.

And it was rammed with people.

"Wow, this is a popular place. Looks like the whole town's come out for a pint," noted Uncle Ernie as we took in the volume of people.

"It sure is crowded. Must be a good magic show." I spied the table the detectives would be using for their show, a simple fold-out table covered in a black cloth with various tools of the trade laid out neatly, the two men deep in conversation. Their top hats and tails were spotless, a crowd eagerly watching from the various picnic benches or standing in groups chatting and laughing while they enjoyed their drinks on this gorgeous Saturday afternoon.

"Is this a common thing in these parts then?" Uncle Ernie removed his black trilby and scratched at his short silver hair, sweat beading on his forehead.

"I don't think so. I've never heard of it before. I think it's just here."

"Bit weird, isn't it? Why are two detectives doing magic?"

"I have no idea. They were really keen for us to come and watch though. They turned up with their costumes on as they'd been practising earlier, and nobody batted an eyelid as everyone's used to it. I guess it's a tradition. Maybe we should go in and get drinks?"

Min stayed with Mum, Dad, and the little guy, who I just knew was silently pleading to have a pack of pork scratchings. Unfortunately, they were way too salty for him, but I promised to get him a nice treat as I'd already spied the sign saying they served doggie ice-cream. I'd noted it had become increasingly popular at many places lately, as businesses at first relaxed their policy on animals being allowed, then actively encouraged them once they realised that a large number of tourists were people with dogs and that was why they holidayed in this country.

The inside of the pub was relatively quiet in comparison to outside, with just a few locals sitting at the bar nursing dark pints of ale, and a few tourists enjoying the comfortable kiosks while they sipped coffees and ate homemade cakes. The ceilings were low in the original pub, with hard-as-iron oak beams, more brass horseshoes than made sense, and ancient photos and artwork gathering dust on the lime-plastered walls. It was a perfect pub, with the smell of cooking and beer soaked into the fabric of the building over centuries.

Beer taps had various local brews showcased, with a few big brands thrown into the mix. Behind the bar, shelves of spirits and glasses hung from racks above the busy staff pulling pints, making coffees, and adding mixers to spirits while waitresses bustled back and forth with trays laden with orders which they took outside through the back I assumed. Open doors meant you could hear the noise from the beer garden, and a pleasant breeze kept the temperature down as the front door was wedged open with an old cast-iron cannonball if I wasn't mistaken.

"Now this is my kind of pub." Uncle Ernie grinned at me and rubbed his hands together, then hurried past the seemingly randomly arranged chairs and stools, Doc Marten's clattering on the dark slate floor. He propped himself up at the bar on his elbows, his bony arms why he'd got the stage nickname Ernie "elbows" as they seemed to have a life of their own and whenever he was performing with his band, the Skankin' Skeletons, he poked them out and went wild.

I joined my uncle and after a bit of salivating over what to choose, and being given samples of a few local ales and ciders, I chose a rather perfect local cider and Uncle Ernie had something called Old Crow's Feet. A dark, thick beer he gushed over but was too bitter for my taste. With the rest of the drinks poured by a harried but polite barman, we took the tray back outside then around to the picnic benches, amazed to discover the others had managed to get a free one.

"You lucked out getting somewhere to sit," I noted as I placed the tray down and eager hands grabbed their drinks.

Anxious whined, looking mournful, until I placed his tub of doggie ice-cream down and he settled under the bench to enjoy his treat.

"A group just left," said Min. "They wanted to stay for the show, but had a few sights they wanted to see before dinner. Lucky, eh?" Min grinned, then sipped her wine and sighed along with everyone else, the drinks ice-cold and perfect on this sweltering afternoon.

"So, fill us in on who's who," insisted Dad.

"Yes, point out the suspects so far, Max," agreed Mum. She downed half her wine, then looked at the glass suspiciously before complaining, "They didn't give me a full glass. Where's it gone?"

"You just necked it, Mum. Slow down. And I'm not going to point to everyone. They'll know we're talking about them."

"But we are talking about them. Which magician is which?" Mum stood and pointed directly at the two men preparing things at the table and taking a sneaky pull of a pint. Judging by the glasses on the table, it wasn't their first either. They sure did things differently around here.

"The taller one is Karl, the other is Monroe. They're both nice guys, and were fine about us looking into this."

"Why wouldn't they be?" asked Dad. "Your wedding got nobbled, and then that mad bint who impersonated the vicar got whacked."

"Bint? Whacked? What are you, a country bumpkin mobster?" asked Mum, frowning at Dad whilst she finished her wine then turned the frown on the glass she upended to check nothing fishy was going on.

"Just stating facts! Anyway, where was I? Ah, yes, why wouldn't Max and Min be allowed to look into things? You can't stop people from talking, and they're great at finding clues and figuring things out." Dad beamed at us both.

Not to be outdone, Mum shoved her empty glass into his hand, so Dad dutifully went to get her a refill, and asked, "Who else is here?"

"There's Ken, the guy from the camping shop. He likes to be called Swede. That's Phil, the blacksmith talking to Mary, the woman who lost her poker. Oh, and there," I nodded in her direction, "is the real vicar. Natasha isn't your conventional vicar, but she has her dog collar on. You can't miss her."

Mum pointed and asked loudly, "That's the vicar? She looks more like a shop keeper."

"Mum, keep your voice down." I hissed. "And what on earth does a shop keeper look like?"

"Her."

"Can't argue with that," I laughed, knowing there would be absolutely no point.

"And there's Hayley," hissed Min, eyes narrowing, face darkening as she spied her nemesis.

We studied Hayley, her red hair like a fire atop her head as the sun lit up her loose curls. Hayley glanced our way, clearly watching us but trying not to make it obvious, but the moment she saw us looking she averted her eyes and lifted her glass of wine to her lips.

"She looks like trouble," noted Mum, gratefully taking her drink from Dad.

"What did I miss?" he asked.

We filled him in as there was no point trying to move on until he was up to speed, then he followed the direction of Mum's finger and agreed, "She does look like trouble. That woman keeps looking at us but pretending not to. And she's got a face on her like a smacked a—"

"I think we get it, Dad," I interrupted hurriedly. "No need for name-calling."

"But you are right," said Min, scowling. "I won't let her spoil our afternoon though."

"Ignore her," said Uncle Ernie. "You don't really think she killed the mystery woman, do you?"

"Not really, no." Min caught my eye, then blurted, "Yes, fine, I do think it was her. She's followed me here, is spying on us, and she vowed she'd get revenge when I dropped her as a client. She's unstable, and I wouldn't put anything past her. We need to be careful."

"Min, love," asked Dad, "how would she get that woman to impersonate the vicar though?"

"I don't know. Maybe she paid her. Maybe she was a friend. Or maybe she had something on her and made her do it. But I'm beginning to believe she's responsible for everything. I might go and talk to her."

"That's not a good idea, love," said Dad, nodding to me.

I nodded in return and suggested, "Let's have our drinks, watch the show, and see what happens. Maybe talk to her later, or maybe not, but don't do it while you're angry. She's not about to admit anything if it was her."

"Sorry, yes, you're right. I'm getting myself worked up when this is meant to be a fun little outing before the party later. Let's relax and enjoy the show."

We turned as Karl and Monroe tapped the table with their wands, both grinning at their captive audience. A hush fell over the entire place as all eyes focused on the men. Clearly, most knew what to expect, and it seemed like everyone was holding their breath. I couldn't imagine what was about to happen, but assumed it would be some sleight-of-hand, or pulling a rabbit from a hat.

Instead, they each took a step away from the other, reached out their hands, nodded, then bent and took a corner of the cloth on the table and whipped it off without disturbing their drinks or the boxes. Everyone clapped, but silence returned almost instantly as the detectives raised the black sheet until it hid them from view.

And then it fell and both men had disappeared!

"They're ghosts!" squealed Mum, and necked her wine to fortify her nerves.

"Don't be daft," shouted Dad to be heard above the raucous round of applause. "They're more like, what's the word? Poltergeists!"

"Or very good magicians," suggested Uncle Ernie.

Mum laughed nervously, Dad patted her hand, then we applauded along with everyone else.

"Over here," shouted someone, and we turned towards the side entrance to the pub where Karl and Monroe were relaxing nonchalantly against the wall, fresh pints in hand, smiling smugly and bowing as everyone cheered.

Min asked me, "How did they do that?" then shook her head in wonder.

Anxious, utterly confounded by the vanishing act, rushed over to the large black cloth and sniffed it nervously. I called for him to come back and not interfere, even though people were laughing and telling him to sniff out how they vanished like that, everyone in good spirits. Karl and Monroe weaved between the picnic benches and groups of people, then bent and had a word with Anxious, the little guy's tail wagging happily the whole time.

Karl bent and picked him up, whispered in his ear, and I was sure he nodded to the man before being put on the table. Anxious stood with his head held high, tail up, back ramrod straight, looking very pleased with himself.

"What are they up to?" whispered Min. "Should we go and get him?"

"I think he's okay. They seem keen to get him involved. Are you worried? I'll get him if you want."

"No, I'm being silly. And he isn't scared."

"Anything but," I laughed, proud of him as he yipped for everyone to pay attention.

"For our next piece of magic," began Karl, "we'll perform a vanishing dog trick with our new best friend, Anxious."

"Aw, what's the matter, little fella?" shouted everyone.

"It's his name, not his emotional state," explained Karl. He glanced our way and winked, then mouthed a silent, "Is this okay?"

Min and I nodded, Mum nicked Dad's pint, and Uncle Ernie took off his hat and rubbed at his head.

Anxious was given the middle of the sheet which he held gently between his teeth, looking rather terrifying with his gnashers bared and his eyes so intent, while Karl and Monroe took a corner each. They raised it up above Anxious' head height, then with a word from Karl, Anxious released the material and it snapped taut, hiding him completely. The little guy barked that he was ready, then the two men nodded to each other and counted down.

"Three, two, one."

The sheet dropped to the ground. Everyone gasped, Mum wailed and emergency drank Dad's beer, Min squeezed my arm in a vice like grip, and my heart fluttered in panic.

"Where is he?" whispered Min, her hold still tight.

"No idea," I admitted, then nearly fell off the bench when Anxious yipped.

There before us, right in the middle of our table, was Anxious, about as proud as any dog could be, head held high, tail spinning so fast it felt like we were in the middle of a storm, a massive grin on his face.

"Anxious!" I reached out as Min released my hand and he jumped into my arms, whining for joy, licking my face and acting like we'd been apart for days, not minutes.

"Good to see you, too, buddy!" I chuckled, then put him back on the table so everyone could make a fuss of him.

The crowd cheered and applauded and he soaked it up, chest swelling, immensely proud of himself.

Karl and Monroe called over to check he was alright, then as the applause died down they got right on with their act, performing some less spectacular but nonetheless impressive tricks from sleight-of-hand, to the traditional rabbit from a hat, and even several bewildering tricks involving levitating guests with their beers. Their grand finale saw them once again hide behind the sheet before dropping it and vanishing.

Everyone applauded wildly as someone from inside the pub shouted, "They're in here, at the bar!"

A moment later, the men appeared at the doorway, pints in hand, took a bow, then retreated to the interior to enjoy their drinks and let everyone discuss how they did what they did. A large group of off-duty officers, and several still in uniform, left their tables or where they were grouped together chatting and retreated into the pub, too, presumably to congratulate their colleagues and continue buying rounds.

"Should they be drinking?" slurred Mum, eyeing the dregs of Dad's pint and licking her lips.

"I guess if they're off-duty it's fine, but it still seems excessive," noted Uncle Ernie, frowning at his finished drink. He brightened, and asked, "Another?"

"Yes please," gushed Mum, handing him her empty wine glass.

Everyone else agreed to another, but I switched to a sparkling water because I was driving, then Uncle Ernie hurried off.

"That was an impressive show." Dad combed his hair nervously, repeatedly checking on Anxious who was curled up and twitching in his sleep, clearly unperturbed by his vanishing act. "Think he's alright? How do they do that?"

"He seems fine, but I have no idea how the trick's done." I turned to Min and asked, "Are you okay?"

"Yes. Um, no. Max, Hayley kept staring at me the whole time. She's up to something. I need to speak to her. I'm getting stressed out, and enough has happened here already. Do you mind?"

"If you think it's for the best, then go and talk to her. Just keep your cool. Shall I come with you?"

"No, I'll go alone. Thanks for offering though. She wandered off down to the stream, so I'll go now. We can talk in private this way." Min stood, brushed down her vest, ran her fingers through her hair, smiled at me, then left.

"She okay?" asked Dad.

"Upset about Hayley being here. Min hates arguments, and doesn't like it if someone thinks badly of her. She's concerned the killer's Hayley."

"They shouldn't be alone then."

"You should go and check on her, Max," agreed Mum, glassy-eyed.

"I'm sure Hayley is just an upset client, but maybe I will wander over to make sure they don't get into a fight."

I left Anxious snoring, sidestepped the benches and groups of people enjoying the late afternoon, then hurried across the open grass and down the bank towards the river.

Min was standing on a small sandy beach beside the slow stream, staring at the body of Hayley face-down in the shallows, her entire head submerged. She waded into the water, and began dragging her out as she screamed, "Somebody help me. Hayley's been murdered!"

Chapter 11

I scrambled down the bank, slid, regained my footing, then splashed into the water as Min tried without much luck to drag Hayley from the shallow stream.

"Get her on her back. Are you sure she's dead?" I blurted.

"I don't know. Maybe. Help me, Max!" Min was shaking badly as we turned Hayley over.

Her face was blue and she wasn't breathing, but she couldn't have been in the water for long. How on earth did she drown anyway? It was so shallow. We pulled her onto the sandy shore by her arms, then I dropped to my knees and readied to perform CPR. I pinched her nose, opened her mouth, checked her airways, then tried to recall the process. I was meant to breathe into her mouth before pumping on her chest, the Staying Alive song giving me the timing I'd been shown.

"I hope this works," I told Min as I turned.

Min's eyes darted to mine, then back down to Hayley's chest. I followed her gaze, then sank back on my knees, knowing that there was nothing I could do to bring her back. A short poker, like the one used to kill the mystery woman, was embedded deeply into the poor woman's chest. Blood trickled from the wound. Mesmerised, I followed its trail as it ran in a rivulet into the water, staining it pink then dispersing, carried away on its slow but inevitable trip to the ocean.

"Max. Max! I didn't even notice it. There's no use giving her mouth-to-mouth. She's gone. Did she drown, or did the poker kill her?"

"The poker, I think, but I don't know. Should I try anything else?"

"Like what? I'm going to get help. Wait here." Min scrambled up the bank and began shouting.

I stood and checked around, but there was nobody else here. Whoever had done this had been fast, and extremely confident, as who commits murder in a field full of coppers? The ground was bone dry, so there was no point checking for footprints, and the sandy shore showed no signs of anyone as it was rather pebbly. Hayley was soaked through, her clothes sticking to her, revealing just how thin she was, and that it was bordering on unhealthy. Min had been right to ask her to stop the extreme dieting, but clearly Hayley had continued. Her red hair fanned out around her blue face, her mouth still open, so I gently closed it by pushing on her chin. She was freezing cold, and felt like plastic, a peculiar sensation that left me staring at my hand as though it held answers, but all I had were questions.

For the briefest of moments, I had an image of Min ramming a poker into Hayley in anger, then it was gone, leaving me stunned. Why would I think that? Obviously, Min wasn't the killer, but my mind was conjuring up terrible images. As I closed my eyes, I even got an image of Uncle Ernie brandishing a poker and ramming it into the shocked Hayley before it was replaced with a terrifying picture of Karl and Monroe in their top hats and tails suddenly appearing from nowhere and Karl killing the defenceless Hayley before they vanished once again.

I shook it off, and got control of my thoughts, then looked at the poker even though it was the last thing I wanted to do. The handle was twisted metal, made from a single length of steel like a miniature version of the one used on the other woman, most likely from Phil's shop and made by him. Why was the killer obsessed with pokers? Who carries something like that around?

There was no time to think of anything else as scores of people came down to the water led by Min. She took my hand and we stepped back as events unfolded, the incongruous sight of Karl and Monroe in their outfits squatting to check on Hayley too surreal for words. Other officers and some of the teams we'd seen earlier crowded around, and Hayley was checked over before they confirmed she was dead. Most of the customers were now either on the tiny beach making it difficult to move, or up on the bank watching. I spied my folks and Uncle Ernie holding Anxious in his arms, the little guy pining to be released so he could join us.

After Min explained to Karl that she'd gone to talk to Hayley but found her in the water, we were told to leave along with everyone else, so the police could check things properly. Stunned, we clambered back up the bank, grateful to be away from the gruesome scene.

"You alright, Son?" asked Dad, putting an arm around me.

"Fine. Shaken up, but okay."

"Come here, love," said Mum softly, and Min stumbled into her arms as Min's shoulders racked and she sobbed.

I rubbed Anxious' chin so he'd settle, then took him from Uncle Ernie who nodded in sympathy and asked, "What happened?"

"I'm not really sure. When I got there, Hayley was in the water, face down, and Min was staring at her then began pulling her out."

"I froze!" Min pulled away from Mum and wiped her eyes, then stepped back so we faced her. "I was angry and went to confront her about why she's been following us, and this time I wasn't going to let her fob me off. She wasn't there, which was confusing, so I slid down the bank to the water, then froze. I was staring at her, doing nothing, then I snapped out of it and began dragging her out and that's when Max arrived. Maybe I could have saved her."

I shook my head and said, "There was nothing you could have done. She was already gone, Min. And you only froze for a second. I was right behind you. It was a massive shock, so of course you paused. Things like this make no sense when you first see them. It takes a moment for your head to figure out what's happening. You did everything you could. The same as I did. We didn't even notice the poker as she was face down and it hadn't gone all the way through like the other one did."

"And nobody else was around?" asked Uncle Ernie, glancing at the throng still watching the police by the stream.

"Nobody," I said. "Min, did you see anyone?"

"It was just me there. And Hayley. Max, what on earth is going on? First all that earlier at our wedding, now Hayley? Do you think she was telling the truth about knowing the area and visiting regularly?"

"I honestly don't know."

"But whatever the reason, why would someone murder her? Who even knew her here apart from us? We're miles from her home, and she came alone, so what exactly is the deal?" With shaking hands on hips, her pitch rose, as if somebody would answer, but we didn't have any answers, just utter confusion.

"You knew the deceased?" asked Karl, appearing with Monroe and several other members of the various teams.

"Yes, I did."

"You didn't mention that just now," said Karl, exchanging a look with his partner.

"Didn't I? There wasn't really time. I was panicked and then you told us to leave. I explained what happened, didn't I? That I found her then tried to get her out and Max helped and was about to perform CPR, then we saw the poker."

"Poker? What poker?" asked Phil. "Nobody told me there was a poker. Was it one of mine? Someone's got it in for me! They're trying to ruin me!"

"Nobody has it in for you, Phil," soothed Karl. "We don't know if it was one of yours. Here, take a look at this photo. Did you make it?" Karl showed Phil his phone and Phil nodded. "So it's yours?"

"That's my trademark spiral. I'd know my own work anywhere. One of the smaller ones, which sell the best as they're cheaper. Tourists love them. I sold loads the last few days."

"You said you'd only sold a few pokers recently," I said, confused.

"Proper ones. These are my baby pokers. More a tourist thing. A memento."

"Min, can we have a word in private?" asked Monroe.

"What? Um, I guess. Why?"

"Just to clear a few things up. Now would be a good time while everything is fresh. Let's get a picnic bench and some privacy. Follow us, please."

"Can I come with you?" I asked.

"I'm afraid not. This is an interview, and it's either here or at the station. I know you're shaken up, but it shouldn't take long. Please just wait."

They led Min through the crowd and we followed behind, watching as Karl spoke to the group at a picnic bench set apart from the others, and they vacated it with their drinks then the three sat down.

"Don't worry, Son, she'll be fine. Min didn't do anything wrong." Dad patted my back, then his arms hung limp by his sides, clearly concerned as he watched Min take a seat.

"I know she didn't, but they're treating her like a criminal."

"Just procedure," said Uncle Ernie. "Relax. It'll be over soon."

"Min's a good girl, so they better be nice," growled Mum, before she smiled at me reassuringly.

"They have to get the details," said Dad, "but the poor girl's shaken up. Max, what's the deal with her and that

Hayley woman? I know you both told us a little earlier, but did Hayley really have it in for Min?"

"It seems that way. I think she most likely did come here to taunt Min. She heard about the wedding thanks to a certain someone who likes to share too much information on the forum he created to talk about the murders I get involved in." I cast a dark look at Dad who merrily ignored the vibe and sipped his pint. "Hayley was trouble, that's for sure, but I can't imagine why anyone would murder her. Then again, she was clearly hard to get along with, so who knows who else she annoyed."

"Plenty of people are annoying, but we don't go around murdering them with pokers right where a load of cops are hanging out on a Saturday afternoon." Dad frowned, then something clicked in his head and he asked me, "Were you talking about me just then? About the forum?"

"Brother, of course he was!" laughed Uncle Ernie, shaking his head at Dad being so slow on the uptake.

"I only update the forum and wiki page because I'm proud of Max and what he does. Fans like to know what he's up to. It seems mean not to share."

"Maybe hold off for a while," I suggested. "We don't want anyone else following us. If you do have to keep talking about the mysteries, maybe wait until they're over so nobody comes and interferes?"

"Good idea. I'll do that. Er, I won't do that. You know what I mean!" Dad flung his arms up in frustration, sloshing beer everywhere.

We soon fell into silence, lost to our thoughts, each of us watching Min being questioned or the various officers and teams setting things up at the crime scene. Hayley was taken away promptly and the area secured, much to the chagrin of the customers, although quite a few seemed excited by the sudden turn of events and were chattering loudly about the murder and how brazen the killer was.

They were right, as this was about the worst possible place to commit such a crime. I thought back over the people I'd seen and how one of them might have been carrying a poker, but knew it was a lost cause. So many people had bags, coats, backpacks, and various items that nearly everyone here had the ability to conceal something if they wished. That obviously meant this was planned in advance, as this wasn't an opportunistic murder unless people were in the habit of carrying pokers around with them.

I couldn't get past that part though. Why a poker? Why two pokers? What was the significance of that? There had to be a reason. Something nobody had figured out, but meant something to the killer. To use such a strange weapon twice meant that whoever did this had their reasons for the way they committed the crime, and that was going to be their downfall. If they'd used something more nondescript, things would make more sense, but I knew from experience that although I didn't know why yet, there was a reason they used them.

"Stop thinking about pokers!" wailed Dad, slapping his hands on either side of his head.

I sighed and asked, "It's not just me then?"

"No, it isn't."

"I'm thinking about them too," said Mum.

"And me," added Uncle Ernie. "It's the most confounding thing. It's like the killer is leaving a massive calling card. A clue so big it's impossible to ignore. But what if that's what they want everyone to think?"

Mum rubbed her hands together and asked, "You mean like a red heron?"

We turned to her, and I couldn't help but ask the obvious. "You mean a red herring?"

"Like a fish? No, I don't think so. A red heron. It means when there's a clue but it's not really a clue, doesn't it?"

"Love, it's called a red herring," said Dad.

"Don't be daft. Whoever heard of a red herring?"

"And who heard of a red heron?" asked Dad.

"Stop teasing. And anyway, that's not the point. Are we saying the killer is trying to trick everyone by making us think that the pokers mean something, when really they don't? That they aren't tied up in this at all?"

"It's a possibility," I conceded. "Trying to divert attention and resources, make everyone get hung up on something insignificant."

"Or," said Mum with a cunning smile, "it does mean something and it's the whole reason why the women are dead." Mum folded her arms, leaned back looking smug, then promptly toppled over backwards as she forgot she was on a bench not a chair.

We jumped up to help, but Dad was beside her first and quickly got her up then stood with his arms out to protect her from view while Mum brushed at her dress, righted her bandanna, pecked Dad on the cheek, then sat down and picked up her drink like nothing had happened.

Stifling our smirks as that would not end well for the Effort men, we rejoined her and took a sip to stop the laughter bubbling over.

"Now, where were we?" asked Mum casually. "Ah, yes, maybe this isn't a red herring at all." She glanced at Dad who nodded that she'd got the word right, then added, "But why use the pokers? If it does mean something, what is that something? Maybe they hate that owner, Phil, or dislike the way he does his blacksmithing, or maybe they're trying to get him into trouble. Or," Mum glanced around before leaning in close to us, "it's Phil and he can't resist using his own creations to murder women. He might be a cereal killer."

I didn't ask, but I was certain that in her head she was thinking *cereal* not *serial*. Some things were best left alone though, so I merely swapped a glance with Dad and Uncle Ernie who were both clearly thinking the same thing.

"Maybe it is a *serial* killer, love," agreed Dad, winking at me.

"Now we just need to figure out the connection between Hayley and the mystery woman," noted Uncle

Ernie. "There must be one, unless this is entirely random, which is a bit of a stretch."

"You're right," I agreed. "There must be a connection. Either Hayley and the other victim knew each other, or someone knew them both and they're linked for some reason we don't yet know. And let's not forget the blindingly obvious."

"Yes?" they asked.

"This is to do with me and Min. It has to be. Ruined weddings, and now Min's stalker dead, means it has to be connected. This is about us."

"You both need to be careful," warned Dad. "We already told you, but you're acting like you're indestructible. What if that'd been Min who was murdered? She was right there just after Hayley was killed. Maybe the killer was after Min really."

"Dad, that doesn't bear thinking about. I can't lose Min."

"None of us want to lose her. That's why I'm saying watch your back. We don't know what's going on, so we have to be cautious."

"So no going off on your own," insisted Mum.

"I can look after myself."

"Nobody can beat a poker through the guts," Dad reminded me.

"True. I'll be careful. Hey, looks like they've finished with Min." I stood as Min nodded to the detectives who then headed off to the crime scene, heads close, discussing the interview I assumed.

"How was it?" I asked when Min returned.

"Fine, but can I please have a drink?"

"Sure. I'll get it," offered Dad, then hurried off.

"You okay, love?" asked Mum. "You look exhausted."

"I'm fine. It's just been a very long day. It feels like we've been here for weeks. But the interview is done, and they were very nice and just wanted the full picture and to know about my history with Hayley. I told them everything, and they said it might be helpful in linking both murders. There must be something in common with both women."

"That's what we were just discussing," I told her. "Did Karl or Monroe have any ideas?"

"No, none. But it's early days, so it's not surprising. They want to talk to Phil, but I think he left."

"Most likely to hurry back to his shop and get every poker he's made on display. Remember, he reckoned he'd sell loads more because of what happened."

"Max, it couldn't be him, could it?"

"Doubtful, as it's very obvious, but if he's unhinged it's a possibility."

Dad arrived and handed Min her drink, so we sat and watched people come and go while we discussed things further, but soon enough it was time to leave.

Chapter 12

The minute we arrived back at the site it was a mad rush to get everything ready. While Min and I peeled, chopped, diced, and finalised what we were actually going to eat, the others set about preparing the marquee, laying out plates and cups, sorting the drinks situation—we might have gone rather overboard with things there, although Mum was doing an excellent job of making a serious dent in the wine. Dad lit a fire in a huge fire bowl Carl and Maureen said they were leaving for the next owners. Apparently, it was made years ago by Phil the blacksmith and they let people use it whenever they wanted, if they could move it to their pitch.

With the fire roaring, and the huge beef stew Min and I had prepared slowly cooking over a smaller fire using the tripod and chain and the massive cast-iron pot I'd rented from the marquee company, all that remained to be done was to check on the stew now and then, watch the fire didn't get too low, and enjoy the atmosphere around the fire bowl.

Once our drinks were poured, we began to relax as the manic energy faded after the rush to get things organised, and we smiled at each other from across the fire, then suddenly everyone burst out laughing.

"Blimey," said Uncle Ernie, "that was intense. I feel frazzled from lugging so much stuff. How many people did you say were coming? What time will they arrive?"

"There aren't loads of guests. We didn't want this to turn into a crazy night with people we hardly know."

"Max, if you'd had your way nobody would be coming at all." Min squeezed my hand and smiled, so I knew she was teasing.

"It's true," I admitted. "Just you guys here is enough, but it will be awesome to catch up with friends we've made over the past year. That's what this is about as much as an excuse to have a party. A way to get everyone together."

"It'll be nice to meet a few of your pals," said Dad. "Anyone we know?"

"Oh, is that Moose guy coming?" squealed Mum. "Have we met him? Didn't he turn up somewhere apart from at the festival?"

"I know Moose," said Uncle Ernie. "He's a great guy and saved the day at the festival. Max figured out who the killer was, but Moose was right in the thick of the action."

"I'm not sure if he's coming or not," I admitted. "I spoke to him, but he's even less chatty on the phone than in person. He said he'd try his best, but couldn't promise anything. But there are some fantastic people coming for certain, so let's make them feel welcome."

"Of course we will," said Mum. "We love meeting people, don't we, Jack?"

"Eh? Yep, love having a natter. What time's dinner, Max?"

"Ages yet. Probably a good few hours. But you've weighed down the table with snacks, and seem to have raided a bakery with the amount or pork pies, sausage rolls, and pasties you bought. It must have cost a fortune."

"Anything for our boy and his new wife," laughed Dad, winking at us. "Just kidding, Min. We've always thought of you as our daughter-in-law, even when you had to give him the boot."

"Um, thank you," giggled Min, squeezing my hand again.

Uncle Ernie cleared his throat and removed his trilby, scratched his scalp, then asked, "Can we discuss something before the guests arrive?"

"What's up?" I asked.

"I think we can agree that something weird is going on around here. I want to be sure that you're taking it seriously."

"We are."

"Of course we are," agreed Min.

"I know you think you are, but maybe you've become too relaxed around murder after dealing with it so often. I'm worried about the pair of you."

"We're being cautious."

"Yes, but Hayley was only just killed and that's put a whole new slant on things. Guys, this is about you. It has to be. First the wedding being faked, the vicar tied up, the woman killed who it seems likely was forced to impersonate Natasha for some reason, then Hayley following Min after their fall out and being killed at the pub. It's getting out of hand. Someone is doing their very best to ruin things."

"But they haven't tried to hurt Max or Min," said Mum, causing us to stare in shock. "What? Did I say something wrong?"

"No, Mum, it's just that usually you're the first one to say we need to watch our backs. You always think that if someone's killed I'm going to be next."

"Well, this time I don't think that. I don't know why that woman pretended to be the vicar, or why she was killed, but I'm not so sure that it was anything to do with you. I think she was going to go through with the fake wedding, but something made her change her mind. I mean, she knew how to do it, didn't she? So it must have been planned well in advance."

"True," agreed Dad. "She knew all the lines, how to perform the ceremony, and had us fooled. You couldn't pull it off if it was something you were forced to do. She planned it, like Jill said."

"Yes, but why?" asked Min.

Mum and Dad shrugged.

"So you don't think this is about us?" I asked Mum.

"No, I do not. I think it's about something we haven't thought of yet. I can't imagine what, but I'm sure you'll figure it out. You always do." Mum sipped her wine, then smiled lovingly at us both, pride in her eyes.

"Thanks, Mum. Uncle Ernie, what do you think now?"

"That you still need to be careful. The one thing we know for certain is that we have absolutely no idea what on earth this is about. So until we do, you should be more cautious than you've ever been."

"We will. Promise."

More conversation was interrupted by the sound of new arrivals shouting hello, so Min and I said we'd go and greet the first of our guests. I smiled as I spied them walking towards us, holding hands, but I stopped dead in my tracks as we got close.

"A baby!?" I shouted, then we hurried forward. I shook Mickey's hand and kissed Sue, then stepped back and grinned at Mickey, looking as proud as any parent could be as he smiled at the baby in the carrier on his chest. The child was fast asleep and utterly angelic.

"You never said you'd had a baby," said Min, kissing them both.

"We thought it would be a nice surprise. And congratulations on the wedding. We were never in any doubt, were we, Sue?"

"Never. You're perfect for each other. Thanks for the invitation."

"Thank you for coming. Um, there's been a slight hiccup with the wedding, but we're still so pleased you could make it."

"I knew it!" Mickey slapped me on the back, then slapped the same hand to his mouth as he'd been shouting.

We remained silent as the baby stirred then yawned and went straight back to sleep. "There's been a murder, hasn't there?" he whispered, grinning from ear to ear.

"Mickey, I thought you were over the whole murder thing? Especially after what I did when we last met Max."

"I am. And don't bring that up now."

"It's water under the bridge," I said, smiling reassuringly at Sue who had thought it would be a good idea to move a body she'd discovered to give Mickey the chance to figure out the mystery of why a naked man ended up in Mum and Dad's horrendous pink rental caravan. "Wow, that feels like so long ago now. How have you both been?"

"Awesome. Still travelling in the van, living the vanlife and loving it. Especially with the weather being so warm and sunny. Max, it's so great to see you. You too, Min. So, fill us in. Who died, and what's this about a wedding hiccup? You haven't changed your mind have you, Max?"

"Mickey, you can't say that. And of course they haven't. Look at them. They're made for each other."

"All in good time," I said. "Maybe we can explain later once the other guests have arrived? Do you want to put the baby down? We have some lovely bell tents for everyone. Um, what about a baby monitor? Do you have one?"

"Course we do, and that would be great. Hey, who's that?" We turned at the rumble of a vehicle, then I spied more coming up the track, so it looked like most of our guests had arrived at the right time and almost together. It would make introductions and getting the party started so much easier this way.

Next to arrive was Dubman, someone who was similar to me in many ways but much more handsome, and he was on fine form as he jumped out of his matt black VW campervan and hugged us before saying anything, a cheesy grin on his face.

Anxious was beside himself now, with so many people to greet and give him a fuss, and Dubman scooped him up and let the little guy lick his beard to get the excitement out of his system, then put him down as Anxious was already keen to greet the next guest. An old friend from Harlech was next to receive his attention, and he tried the old poorly paw trick, much to Erin's delight.

Next was a couple I'd spent a few weeks with after the Christmas debacle, and before we even had a chance to speak some of my newest buddies arrived, looking cheery but tired. A lovely woman named Bonnie and her twin daughters who I'd spent quite a lot of time with recently squealed as they spotted Anxious and he wagged for joy at seeing so many friends again.

Of course, there were plenty who couldn't make it, but it was heartening going through my contacts and realising just how many people I'd met and spent time with over the last year. It was easy to miss staying in touch, but having the wedding was a great excuse to call people and catch up on news, all of us vowing to be better at calling regularly, but even if we didn't we were friends for life. It warmed my heart to know that all around the country were those I could rely on and they could do the same, and the checklist of who to call had been surprisingly long.

Now the party could get under way, as everyone who had said they could come was here, but I was rather sad that Moose hadn't turned up. Knowing him, he was already at the party and had slipped in without us even being aware. That would be his style.

A flurry of greetings, hugs, snatched conversation, and plenty of laughs followed before Min and I asked if everyone would follow us back to the fire where we'd explain what'd been happening and hopefully get the party going properly. I introduced Min to those she didn't know, but it came as a shock to both of us how many she'd already met. I couldn't help teasing her about how often she'd come to stay, even though she'd wanted time apart to come to terms with everything.

The introductions took much longer once back at the pitch, because Mum and Dad weren't ones to just say hi then move on to the next person. We got there eventually, though, then with everyone gathered around the fire with drinks in hand, and the baby fast asleep in the bell tent, I reluctantly had to put a downer on the mood by explaining as quickly as I could what had happened and that in fact we hadn't even got married at all.

Nobody minded that we weren't married, and were very understanding, but shocked by the murders and the peculiar circumstances. Min promised she still wanted to get married despite there seeming to be a sinister plan to break us apart, which lightened the mood, so after we'd finished recounting the tale, with a few helpful words from the two fifties fanatics, I asked if we could not talk about it any more and just get down to the serious business of having fun.

With a rowdy cheer, and me being grateful for the fact the site was closed as otherwise we'd be that annoying group at a campsite making too much noise and ruining the peace for others, that's exactly what we did. Uncle Ernie rushed behind the decks and played some belting tunes of all genres to keep everyone happy, even Mum and Dad, and Min and I even had the first dance just like if we'd been married. Once Uncle Ernie said a few words over the mike, he turned up the volume and things got rather wild rather quickly. Seemingly, everyone was keen to party, with all guests having a tale to tell about how the year had been hard, in some cases less than fun, and they wanted to let their hair down.

I was grateful for so many friends making it, especially as this wasn't exactly local for most, and as the night wore on and we got caught up in talking and laughing, I almost fainted when I realised I'd completely forgotten about the food!

With a tight lump in my throat, I rushed over to the pot, the smells enticing and no burning I could note, sure that the delay would only make the stew even better as I'd set it on a very low heat so it could cook to perfection. When I lifted the lid and was greeted with a face full of steam, my panic subsided and I couldn't help but smile as I inhaled.

Feeling like Kane from Kung Fu, although I did use oven gloves, I hauled the pot from the hook, carefully placed it on the ground, then poked the fire until I was satisfied and loaded up the huge paella pan. Maybe it was the smells, or maybe everyone was simply famished and in search of food, but soon I had an audience as I oiled the pan, added the stock, and began the labour-intensive process of cooking the paella rice while the stew finished cooking off the heat.

Once the rice was cooked, and with everyone pitching in to help prep what was needed, we took turns adding the various meats, prawns, and vegetables, which I finished with some extra seasoning.

Dad and Dubman took the paella dish over to the marquee, while Min helped me with the huge pot of stew, guests following in our wake, joking about being careful not to drop it as everything smelled amazing. I couldn't stop smiling, as this was what life was all about. Food, friends, fun, and fooling around. The atmosphere was buzzing, with everyone getting on so well even though nobody had known each other a short while ago.

Min and I settled the pot carefully on the floor as I feared the table would collapse, and everyone helped sort out the various breads and sides, along with olives and a selection of cold cuts, salads, pasta dishes, and all manner of interesting treats, then it was finally time to eat. I ladled out stew while people helped themselves to the paella, then rather than sit we gathered around the fire as the sky darkened, and tucked in.

The sound of people eating always brought a smile to my face, knowing that they appreciated the work you'd put in, and today was no exception. I couldn't help grinning as I spooned mouthfuls of delicious stew into my mouth, and sampled the paella which was cooked to perfection.

Dad called for silence, then became bashful for a moment as everyone looked at him, then simply said, "To Max and Min. I love them both, and wish them nothing but happiness and long lives together. Cheers."

"Cheers!" shouted everyone, then began congratulating us on being together if not married, then me for the food, before tucking back in with gusto.

"That was some accomplishment," said Dubman as he came over. "How do you do it, Max?"

"I spent years cooking fancy food in restaurants, so large dishes like this are a breeze."

"Yes, but how do you make it taste so amazing? I can cook, but whatever I do it never tastes as good as that,"

"Max has the knack," said Min. "It's infuriating. He's never made a bad meal in his life. It's so unfair. I can copy everything he does but it still doesn't taste as incredible."

"You're a great cook," I said, nodding my thanks, knowing I was grinning rather manically because of the kind words and the atmosphere.

"Thanks for inviting me," said Dubman. "It's been liberating to let my hair down. I needed this. St David's is a stunning place, but the winter's get bleak. I moved around more than usual, and have had some great times, but it's awesome to catch up with you again and to meet some new friends."

"We're glad you could make it. Is everything okay?"

"Yeah, fine, but sometimes vanlife gets lonely, you know? It happens to us all. Some years are fantastic, others are more of a drag. If I get a few quiet weeks without speaking to many people, I feel in a funk, so this was exactly what I needed."

"Dubman, come and dance with me," asked Erin, her nose piercing and earrings glistening in the orange glow of the fire, then dragged him off before he could even answer.

"This is a special night," said Min, cuddling up close to me.

"It sure is. Perfect. Especially as we're together. Come on, let's go and dance."

Chapter 13

The party went on late into the night, with friends new and old laughing, chatting, and dancing. There was even the hint of a new romance between Dubman and Erin. Mickey and Sue were the first to call it a day as their baby left them constantly exhausted. Mum and Dad, to everyone's astonishment apart from mine and Min's, were still going strong at 1AM, and refused to let Uncle Ernie wind down the sound system. Finally, everyone retreated to their tents, leaving me alone with Min for what felt like the first time in days.

As we finished stacking the last of the cups, Min grabbed me and planted a very wet kiss on my lips.

"What was that for?"

"For being a wonderful man. For making the party perfect. Wasn't it great?"

"It sure was. So you had a good time? Weren't put off by what happened?"

"Max, I had the best time ever. It was a fabulous party. I know lots of people, mostly my bunch of awful family and some of your new friends, couldn't make it, but maybe it was better because it stayed quite small. Everyone got on so well and was so nice. They even helped clean up."

"It got it done much quicker. Min, I'm so lucky to have you in my life."

"And I feel the same, but right now all I want to do is sleep. You coming to bed?"

"In five. I want to take a wander around, just to clear my head, but I promise I'll be there soon. If there's any room left on the bed. Anxious crashed out hours ago, so will be spread-eagled and snoring."

With a giggle, then a yawn, Min declared, "I don't care. I'll sleep on top of him if I have to."

Alone, I soaked up the silence without moving for a while, then walked around the perimeter of the small field before heading back up the track into the larger one, picturing what the site would look like full of happy campers, the bright moon affording enough light to imagine it perfectly. The stream gurgled the other side of the hedge, a soothing, lulling background noise to the wind rippling gently through the trees. A rabbit hopped past, almost right in front of my feet, and I had to stifle a laugh as I knew Anxious would be annoyed if I told him he'd missed out.

After following the hedge line, I cut across the dewy grass and up past the old toilet block, still serviceable but in dire need of a total revamp if not demolition and a rebuild. The outbuildings came next, staggered along the track up to the house like drunken monoliths, all at different angles to each other but beautiful under the moon's silver haze. A few lights for guests remained on, but most didn't work. How much would it cost to run new heavy-duty electric cables and get the site sorted? An absolute fortune, I assumed.

At least the lights at the house still worked. The wall and gate were lit up in a pleasing glow from the two lights embedded in the wall. I stopped in my tracks, though, when I thought I heard a noise from the side of the house hidden from view, my ears straining. When I heard nothing more, I crept forward slowly, my heart hammering, Uncle Ernie's warning now feeling like very sensible advice. What was I doing wandering around alone in the dark at almost 2AM? This was foolish.

Nevertheless, I continued, wondering if I should call someone to tell them or leave them asleep. This was silly. I was merely letting my imagination run wild. Most likely, it was another rabbit, or maybe a fox come to investigate the noise and hope to snaffle some scraps, although I'd been fastidious about cleaning everything away. Leave no trace had been a good motto to follow ever since I began vanlife, and it was ingrained now.

A door clicked shut, an almost imperceptible snap of the lock catching after the whoosh of the sliding doors running on well-oiled tracks. Someone was breaking into the house. Acting sensibly, I pulled out my phone and was about to dial 999 when a light clicked on in the back, a warm glimmer seeping around to the side path. A stretched, angled shadow was cast as someone stepped out from the rear, nothing but a silhouette, the light behind them.

I shook my head to clear my mind as it was definitely playing tricks on me as this figure was huge, a true giant.

"Max, what are you doing here?" asked a familiar voice.

I sighed, trying to calm my fast-beating heart, and chuckled inwardly as I pocketed my phone. "Frankie, what's going on? It's two in the morning. Where's your vehicle? I didn't see anything."

"I left it in the passing point just before the gate. Didn't want to disturb anyone at this ungodly hour. And, er, well, I'm spooked to be honest. I heard about the murder this afternoon, got told while I was driving here, and thought it best to keep a low profile. Didn't want anyone to know I was here so I couldn't get killed." Frankie chuckled nervously and wrung his hands, his voice quivering.

"Fair enough. But why are you here at all? Are your folks with you?"

"No way. They're tucked up in bed and fast asleep."

"Are Carl and Maureen alright? Did the move go well?"

"Fine. But Mum misses the place a lot already. They spent so long here, and it holds so many memories for us. I love it here, Max, but it's time to move on. I hope it goes to someone who feels the connection to it the same as we do."

"You never fancied running the business?"

"I have my own business and a family to look after. This isn't for me. And besides, it's theirs, not mine."

"But you wished it was yours?" Did I hear a tinge of bitterness in his voice?

"Sometimes. At least I did when I was younger. Now I'm old enough to admit that this life isn't for me. I enjoy my creature comforts and a garden that's easy to maintain. Never have the time or energy for much after work."

"I guess you'll inherit the money from the sale at some point?" I asked, knowing it was a blunt question but feeling very uncomfortable. I kept a tight hold on my phone, the number already dialled in, just the green send button to call the police.

"One day, but my parents will be around for years yet. I have my own thing going on and do alright, so it isn't an issue. It will be nice, of course, but I'd rather have them close by and enjoy life rather than struggle here."

"Which brings us back to why are you here?"

"Max, I'm not sure I appreciate your tone. In case you've forgotten," Frankie stepped forward, allowing me to get a clear view of him, "my family still owns this site. Mum and Dad were gracious enough to let you stay for your party, but you don't own it. We do."

"Sure, of course. It's just that you're sneaking around in the middle of the night, dressed all in black, and you took me by surprise."

"I'm in black as these are my clothes. Nothing suspicious about it. And I'm not sneaking. I'm being mindful of other people so didn't want to disturb anyone. I could ask you the same question. What are you doing up here at this time? Shouldn't you be at your party or asleep?"

"I wanted to clear my head, and to take a look around while it was quiet. It's a beautiful place."

"It sure is. Look, let's start again. I think we're both on edge. I almost didn't come after I got the call saying what happened this afternoon, but Mum was freaking out about forgetting a few things so I told her I'd make the drive. It's a crazy long trip, and I've been on the road so much today, but I have work tomorrow as everyone wants to move on the weekend, so haven't got any other time to do this."

"I understand. Sorry about the misunderstanding. Anything you need a hand with?"

"Nothing much. Just a few personal items they forgot. Trinkets really. It's sorted now. I was just taking a final look around now it's mostly emptied. I miss it here. Sometimes when I was younger I used to get up in the middle of the night and wander around, pretend I was a ninja. It got so busy here in the summer, and I'd sneak round the tents, having the best time. Happy days. Actually, maybe that is why I'm wearing black. Trying to be a ninja again. Bit harder now as I never stopped growing. Now I get spotted a mile away." Frankie laughed at the memory, but it faded fast and was replaced with a wistful look.

"You love the campsite, don't you?"

"Sure do. Simpler times. Being a kid with all this space was awesome. I got to meet so many people and everyone was happy as they were on holiday. It was a great way to grow up. Now I'm in the burbs with my own family and sometimes I wonder if this kind of life would be better for the kids. But I know myself well enough to know it isn't for me."

"I'm sure you could always come and visit. Maybe come as a guest rather than the owner."

"That's a great idea! Maybe I will, as long as no developer gets their hands on it and turns it into something monstrous."

"It's too nice a place for that. Why, have you heard something?" Inexplicably, I began to sweat picturing this beautiful spot turned into a corporate campsite or worse, everything demolished and houses built.

"People have been sniffing around for years. The large companies wanted to incorporate the site into their portfolios. Mum and Dad always said no and even now are insisting it won't go to anyone who wants to destroy the feel of the place. Sure, it needs a ton of money spending to sort out the house, which will be eye-watering, and the whole site needs a massive revamp, so we'll have to see, I guess." Frankie shrugged, almost like he was defeated and knew the inevitable would happen.

"This is the real reason you came, isn't it? To visit one last time without your parents here? To remember the good times and see it while it's quiet?"

"I guess. I hadn't thought about it like that, but I suppose you're right. Well, it's time to go. I have an epic drive, then it will be straight to work. No sleep for me tonight. Enjoy your stay." Frankie approached, then we shook, his large hands still soft, and slightly damp.

I heard the gate clang shut, then a car start, and caught the headlights shining on the hedges before he turned then was gone, leaving me alone in the silence.

"Was it me, or was that weird?" I asked the night. "Why was he really here? How long has he been here?" I couldn't help but feel uneasy about Frankie's covert nighttime visit. Whatever explanation he gave, it was beyond odd to drive so far after already being here yesterday. He'd have hardly got home and settled his parents before he'd made the return trip. It would take hours. And for trinkets? But there was no way he could have killed the two women, was there? He was with the owners yesterday afternoon, unless they hadn't left when I thought they had and he'd dropped them somewhere while he did the deed, then took them.

Things were definitely getting out of hand. I was trying to read too much into things and overreacting to Frankie's presence when I should have taken his explanation at face value. Nevertheless, I wandered around to the back and checked the doors were locked and there was nothing weird going on, before returning to the front of the house.

From nowhere, a figure emerged from right beside the front door. I hadn't noticed him at all, but as he stepped forward the man wearing boots, combat trousers, and a black hoodie barred my path.

"Moose! You made it."

"Hello, Max. Sorry if I startled you." Moose grinned, his cherubic face and soft voice at odds with his large frame; I'd taken to him the moment we'd met. Overweight, and matching me in height, he was a large, intimidating presence, but one of the nicest guys you could hope to meet. He was also a ninja, or as close to it as you got, and had astounded me and Min with his swift movements, ability to seemingly vanish then appear at will, and had played a crucial role in unravelling the murder mystery at the music festival.

"It's been a strange day, but it's great to see you. You're very late for the party though."

"It was a long trip, and I had a few things to do along the way, but I didn't want to miss seeing you both. I hear it didn't go as planned."

"How did you hear?" I asked, not surprised he knew all about it.

"You know me. I know most things that are going on. Was it a good party?"

"The best."

Moose nodded, seemingly having used up all the words he had, and now I thought about it this was probably the most he'd ever spoken to me in one go. He stepped back against the wall, somehow managing to blend in with the stone and shadow until it made me feel dizzy and I had to really focus to keep him in my sight and thoughts. Once again, I wondered who this guy was and how exactly he did what he did. As if sensing my unease, Moose moved forward, gliding like he was no more solid than the breeze drifting lazily past us.

"I wish you'd teach me that," I laughed.

"It took me years, and I still practice all the time. Max, that Frankie man didn't give off good vibes."

"No, he didn't. You were here for that? You heard what we said?"

"I saw and heard everything. He's not the killer, I don't think, but he wasn't being honest either."

"What do you think he was doing here?"

"I have no idea," Moose admitted with a shake of the head. "Maybe it means nothing. Maybe he forgot something personal. A childhood keepsake."

"Moose, my friend, let's get back to the field and chat. We've got plenty to catch up on."

"You need to rest. I need to rest. I walked for a day, and half the night to get here."

"You didn't come by car? Do you own one? Where do you live, Moose?" Maybe this time I'd get some answers from him.

"I own nothing and I own everything. I live here and I live there, and I travel in many ways."

"Suit yourself," I said, smiling, as he remained as elusive and secretive as ever. "But come and have a drink with me."

"Tomorrow. Tonight, I have things to do then I must sleep. See you soon, Max." Moose glanced past me and I turned to look, then quickly spun around to find he was gone.

The memory of the encounter was already fading, and I had to focus incredibly hard to remember our conversation, but at least I did. The last few times we'd met, nobody else ever recalled Moose apart from me, Min, and Uncle Ernie, and now I understood why. Somehow, he could make himself fade from people's memory like a ghost thought. Here, then gone.

Exhausted, and confused by the two encounters, I wandered back across the campsite and opened the door to Vee quietly, removed my Crocs, then forwent trying to undress in the tiny patch of floor space not taken up by the bed and simply squeezed in beside Min and Anxious. My buddy opened an eye, sniffed, then seemingly satisfied dropped straight back to sleep. Min didn't stir once.

I drifted off to sleep and dreamed of ninjas attacking the van, surrounding us on all sides and ready to pounce. I woke instantly in a cold sweat, checked we were alone in the campervan, then finally sank into a dreamless sleep as I wondered what the day would bring. Would we catch ourselves a killer, or have to leave without ever knowing the truth of the peculiar events of the previous day.

The moment I woke up, it was like something had changed. I felt recharged, strangely wired, and ready to push this thing forward. I made a mental checklist of things to do, people to speak to, and leads to follow up on, and was itching to get started. Min and Anxious were gone, and I could hear people outside talking in low voices, so I got changed, then opened the door, ready to face another day.

Chapter 14

"Hey there, sleepyhead." Min looked as fresh as if she'd had an early night, her light make-up applied, hair bouncing like it was full of sunshine, cheeks glowing, her tanned arms and legs on show.

"Morning. Wow, you look beautiful. Have you been up long?"

"About an hour. Sorry if I disturbed you."

"I didn't hear a thing. It's a stunning day already."

"Sure is. I didn't want to miss it. It's going to be boiling, so be sure to put on sunscreen."

"I will. First, I need to use the facilities." I kissed Min, gave Anxious a fuss as he trotted over and sat, hope in his eyes, but I told him it was very early for treats so he lay down and grumbled to himself, causing me to smile.

As I wandered over to the toilet and shower blocks, I spied a few people up and outside their bell tents, but most were still asleep. I waved, and said good morning, but didn't stop to chat, and hurried to my destination trying not to look like the man desperate for a pee that I was.

Feeling better, I took a more leisurely walk back to the van, stopping to chat with Mickey and Sue and see how the baby was doing. Little Maximus, which I was honoured to hear was named after me, was gurgling and waving his arms around, so I said a proper hello now he was awake and held him so he could play with my hair. He had a strong grip and didn't want to let go until Sue gently prized his chubby fingers open and took him from me.

Dubman was up, too, and as I waved hello I spied Erin emerging from her own tent and instantly making a beeline for him.

"I'll leave you to it," I said with a nod in her direction.

"Thanks, man. She's a great gal. I know we only met yesterday, but there's a real connection there."

"Then good luck."

Mum and Dad were nowhere to be seen, and judging by their energetic dancing I assumed they'd be asleep for a while yet as it was only just gone eight. I hurried past in case Mum emerged and started interrogating me on where I'd been, and reached our pitch unscathed and un-Mumified.

Min handed me a coffee the moment I returned; I sipped on the bitter liquid gratefully. It was strong, with a splash of milk, and exactly what I needed to dissipate the last of the fog in my head. I told her about the encounters last night, and she seemed to think that Frankie was most likely on the level as there was no possible way he could have committed the murders unless he could be in two places at once, but I wasn't so sure.

I argued that he could certainly have killed the mystery woman as he didn't turn up at the campsite until much later, and he could have left his parents somewhere while he returned to kill Hayley, but Min made a very good point of reminding me that nobody had seen him at the pub. Whoever killed Hayley must have been there, so they would have been seen. It was one thing to kill her, quite another to have managed it without anyone noticing him there.

It eased my nerves, although in a way I wished it was Frankie as then at least we'd know where we stood. When I explained about Moose, she grew very excited, but was disappointed when I told her about his vanishing act.

"He's so mysterious. Why did he come so late then just disappear?"

"He said he walked and it took him all day and the night too. He wouldn't tell me if he had a house or anything, the same as always."

"He's been like that since we met him. A real man of mystery. He's only young too. Did he say if he's still working as a security guard?"

"We didn't discuss it."

"Think he'll turn up today?"

"Your guess is as good as mine. He said he had a few things to do."

"Oh, that's a shame. I like Moose."

Anxious must have woken up and been listening, as at the mention of Moose's name he shot up, sat, looked around, then whined.

"You like him, too, don't you?" I teased. "Is he one of your favourite people?"

Anxious barked; I had my answer.

"Do you think he's okay?" Min chewed her bottom lip and played with her hair.

"I think so, but who knows? With Moose, anything is possible. I'm sure he's fine, but it would be nice to have a proper chat with him. Min, I was thinking that we should go back into town and speak to people. Maybe catch up with the detectives too. What do you think? Is it rude? I know most people are heading home today, but maybe we should stick around."

"We should spend some time with them this morning and see what everyone's plans are. We can't go yet after how far they've travelled."

"You're right, so let's cook a nice breakfast for everyone, then see what happens."

With so much great bread left over, I decided to make a simple breakfast of scrambled eggs with all the extras and toast the bread over the coals of the large fire, which were still baking hot. People emerged from tents or brought their coffees to congregate at the marquee, and we chatted about the party and caught up on any news we hadn't shared the day before while I diced ham, chopped peppers and onions, grated cheese, and even threw in a few prawns and a selection of meats, deciding that after several dozen eggs would be added I'd best switch and use the paella pan.

Dad, dressed to impress, did the toast while Mum finished getting ready for the day, as no way would she be seen by so many people unless she was immaculate. Once everything was ready, and just in time, she made an appearance looking as well made-up as always. Today, her red hair was tied back by a purple bandanna to match the purple polka dots on her utterly impractical white flared dress. It went without saying that the shoes matched.

She beamed with pride at the compliments from the others, so we settled down at the picnic benches and enjoyed a breakfast feast then everyone discussed their plans for the day. I already knew Mickey and Sue had somewhere to be, so they would be leaving soon, and although Dubman had planned on leaving, too, an invitation from Erin to return to Harlech with her so she could show him around was too great an offer for him to refuse. The twins, who had crashed before midnight the previous night, were still exhausted and Bonnie apologised and explained that she had to get back home by early afternoon for a shift at the deli. Maddie and Roy, the couple I'd stayed with after the Christmas corpse debacle, were heading home too. They still had an epic amount of work to do at their campsite, but I got a lot of great information from them about how to run a business, and they promised to stay in touch more regularly.

With no answer from Moose, that meant our guests apart from family would be gone by late morning, so in the meantime we set about cleaning up after breakfast then returned to Vee and sat outside the gazebo and soaked up the morning sun. It gave us another opportunity to enjoy this tranquil spot, and we both savoured the time together while we watched everyone sort out their things. It was a shame everyone's visits were so brief, but sometimes that's the way the cards fall, and it made me appreciate the effort they'd made even more.

Sitting and relaxing helped put yesterday's calamities into perspective. We might not be married, but it sure felt like it. We were alive, and together, surrounded by friends and family, so we had absolutely nothing to complain about. Hayley might not have been a nice person, but nobody deserved what happened to her, or the other woman. I knew that if we could figure out who she was, things would start to make sense, so wanted that to be a priority. Where to start?

I decided to let things play out as they might, and stop forcing the issue, so sank low in my chair, felt the familiar uncomfortable bar of the camping chair across my legs, and smiled happily to myself. This was the life. Outdoors, a fancy gazebo to triple the size of the van, Min beside me wiggling her red-painted toes in the grass, Anxious snoring, and my beloved campervan right behind us, as much a part of the family as everyone else.

By late morning, Mickey and Sue were ready to leave. They apologised again as they'd planned on staying another night but friends they'd promised to meet with had an emergency so they were going to babysit while they went to the hospital to deal with a parent's untimely admission.

Dubman explained that he didn't want to be a gooseberry and was leaving today so we didn't feel obliged to hang out with him, but I insisted that it would have been great for him to stay. But with the invitation from Erin, we understood why he was going too. And Erin had work at the vets, which I was pleased to hear was doing better than ever, so she couldn't stay even though she wanted to.

We said our goodbyes, everyone promising to meet up again soon, maybe to actually celebrate our wedding next time, then the site emptied and the sound levels dropped. Min and I decided to take Anxious for a stroll through the woods over a stile that had a clever pull up section so dogs didn't have to try to jump over or be picked up by their owners. It was rather rickety, and needed replacing, but I appreciated that Carl and Maureen had been so considerate of their guests.

The moment we were over the stile and the other side of the hedge, the silence of the forest engulfed us. The cool air was a delight, and I laughed as I shivered, amazed how much difference the cover from the trees made. The meandering stream gurgled over mossy rocks, soaking up the sides of the banks covered in ferns and tiny wild white flowers.

Untouched by human hand for decades, the forest floor was littered with rotten fallen branches and mossy stumps where trees had inevitably died or been damaged by storms. Moss crept over everything, making the going soft and slow, which suited us just fine as it gave us the chance to soak up the incredibly calm atmosphere. Anxious was in his element, chasing along trails made by rabbits, foxes, and possibly deer, yipping occasionally before racing back, panting, and taking a sip of water from tiny pools in hollows.

Gnarly old oak and broad beech mixed with hawthorn and soaring ash, yew, hazel, and a gigantic sycamore that blocked the sun, while slender saplings grew tall and whiplike as they tried to reach the light. A path led up then around the incline, but it was faint now after not being used for several years by any guests.

"What's that?" was the first word spoken by either of us since we entered, and Min pointed to something snagged on a snapped branch up ahead.

"Let's go and see."

Taking it slow as the path was littered with branches and roots that could easily twist an ankle, we made it to the tree and stopped. Hanging on the broken branch was a striped red and once white cotton bag without branding. It had clearly seen better days and was beginning to rot.

"I wonder what's inside?" mused Min. "Think it's okay to look?"

"I don't see why not. Whoever hung it there did so a long time ago. Maybe it was dropped and someone found it, so put it there hoping that if anyone came searching they'd see it."

"I'm going to take a peek." Min reached out and lifted a handle from the tree and we both peered inside. Frowning at each other, she reached in and pulled out a tiny pair of red leather shoes. They must have been for a child under one as far as I could tell, with little laces still tied in neat bows.

"Is there anything else?"

Min took the bag down completely and checked, but there was nothing else. "That's it. Just shoes. Why would someone be carrying baby shoes in a bag?"

"No idea. Maybe they took them off a child then dropped them. Maybe a gift? Who knows?"

"Max, this is weird and spooky. You don't do any of those things. Who carries only shoes in a bag? This is freaking me out."

"Min, it's nothing to worry about. The bag's been here for years, and I'm sure that the only thing that happened was someone, possibly a couple, were here with their baby and they got hot feet. They took the shoes off, pulled a bag out of a massive backpack as you need so much stuff for kids, then dropped it. Some kind soul hung it up and it was never found. End of story."

"Do you really think that's what happened?" Min brushed at her face and smiled sadly, then hung the bag back up.

"Sure. Hey, it's alright. What's got into you? Don't get upset."

Anxious raced back, tongue lolling, and yipped loudly as he sat and wagged, head cocked. When he realised Min was sad, he pawed at her leg until she bent and picked him up, then he licked her salty cheeks, convinced it would make everything better.

"Thank you, Anxious. That was just what I needed," Min sniffed, then smiled weakly at me before lowering the little guy and telling him he could go and play again. He glanced at me, and I nodded, so he raced off back up the track in search of prey he'd never catch.

"This hit you very hard, didn't it?"

"Sorry, I'm being silly. The shoes made me sad, and I thought that maybe something bad had happened to a child."

"I don't think that's the case, Min. I'm sure that whoever these belonged to is much bigger now and driving their parents crazy. Come on, let's go and find Anxious. Aren't you keen to explore the rest of the woods?"

"Sure I am. We shouldn't take too long, though, as we promised to have lunch with everyone then return to town. I wonder if the detectives have uncovered anything yet."

"Let's hope so. I'd like to call in on the vicar. See how she's doing."

"That's a good idea."

"Hey, we haven't even explored the lake yet, but that's on the other side up above the house I think. Maybe another time?"

"Maybe, but we have to leave tomorrow, so we might not get the chance. Max, I don't want to go. It's so beautiful here. Think they'd mind if we stayed?"

"I'm not sure, but the place goes up for sale tomorrow, remember, so they'll be showing people around."

"I hope Frankie isn't right and a developer snaps it up."

"I doubt they will. It's too remote for them to build many houses, but one of the chain camping companies will be interested for sure. Carl and Maureen don't want that, which is why they offered it to us."

"It would be dreamy, wouldn't it?"

"Very."

"But it isn't vanlife, is it?"

"Not exactly," I laughed. "We haven't had the chance to discuss it properly, but would you like to take on a project like this? Live somewhere like this? You quit your job to travel with me and Anxious, but this would be a lot of hard work."

"I'd do it if you wanted to. It's dreamy, and I adore the site, the barns, and even the house. Not that I fancy living in a house again. Certainly not yet. I love being in Vee and moving around."

"It's a huge step, isn't it? We haven't talked about doing something like this before."

"Isn't that the beauty of life? That sometimes the best things are the ones you never even considered? Who thought you'd be a vanlifer?"

"I certainly didn't. I imagined I'd be in sweaty kitchens getting annoyed about sauces until I finally keeled over from exhaustion or plain annoyance at letting myself get so taken over by my obsessions."

"And yet here we are, solving mysteries, walking in the woods, and still not married." Min smiled, then kissed me as she squeezed my hand.

"Not yet, but if there's one thing I can promise it's that we will be husband and wife again."

"I believe you."

We continued up the track until it grew faint then vanished, but there was still plenty of woodland left to explore. We agreed it could wait for another day, so turned around and headed back to the campsite slowly, enjoying the cool air as we moved deeper into the shade again.

Min was silent as we passed the bag, and I don't know why but I turned and raced back then took it down and put it into my satchel.

Min raised an eyebrow but didn't ask any questions. I had no answer for her anyway.

Chapter 15

"You're that man," accused Mary, lifting her walking stick and pointing it at me, her balance seemingly fine hefting the heavy looking gnarly stick with ease. Another one of Phil's creations who was seemingly as expert with wood as he was with metal.

Bemused, I glanced at Min, then my uncle and parents, and asked, "I am?"

"Yes," she snapped. "And you're that woman."

"Who me?" asked Mum, frowning in confusion.

"No, not you. Her!" Mary prodded Min in the stomach with the walking stick, causing her to squeal.

"So you're saying I'm not a woman?" asked Mum, now utterly out of her depth.

"She is," said Dad. "Don't you go accusing my wife of not being a woman. I can tell you for a fact she is. You should see her without her—"

"I know what a woman is," growled Mary, nudging a silent man standing beside her. He flinched as Mary told him, "Are you going to let her speak to me like that?"

"Which one, Mum? And nobody said anything bad. Excuse Mum," he said to us, spreading his hands and sighing, "she's having a rough few days."

"I forgot Mary had a son," I said, wondering why I felt put out for not recalling. "I think Phil mentioned it, but we haven't seen you around."

"Mum likes to pretend she's this helpless old lady living alone in squalor, when the truth is that I look after her and she looks after me. I might be fifty, but sometimes it feels like she's the carer, not me."

"I don't need caring for. I'm as fit now as I was in my thirties," hissed Mary, waving her stick around, the muscles in her thin arms as taut as the skin.

"But you like to hobble about and pretend you're frail."

"Sometimes my hip hurts," she admitted. "And my shoulder."

"That's because you keep waving that huge walking stick around. I told you to get a lighter one, Mum."

"I like the heft. Makes me feel protected from bullies."

"What bullies?" I asked, intrigued. "Have you been having issues?"

The son glared at Mary and told us, "Mum likes to exaggerate. There are no bullies around here."

"No, but there are killers." Mary shivered, clutching her stick tight.

"Yes, well, that's not normal, is it? Hi, I'm Arnold. Sorry to hear about what happened. It's a small town so news travels fast, and we have the main gossip right here."

Mary slapped her cane against Arnold's legs and said, "I do not gossip."

"Watch it with that, Mum. I've warned you before." Arnold rubbed at his thigh then smiled, but it looked forced, and as though he'd like nothing better than to rip the stick from his mother's hands and throw it away.

"It's been a peculiar few days," I admitted. I introduced everyone, curious about this man. He was rather an odd-looking guy with obviously dyed black hair slicked back like Dad's but thinning rather than the full head of hair he was so proud of. He was wiry, just shy of six foot, and wore plain black chinos, tatty trainers, and a very crisp white shirt which I meanly assumed his mother ironed for him. Of all things, he wore a rather retro and stylish lightweight green parka with a fur-trimmed hood and orange lining. How he wasn't sweating was astonishing as the temperature had soared to the high twenties, meaning Min and I were in shorts and vests although Uncle Ernie and my folks wore their usual garb, and always had no matter the weather. Sometimes being a slave to fashion had its downside, but at least the rest of us had bare arms and could breathe in our clothes.

"I hear you're quite the amateur sleuth?" asked Arnold, craning his long neck forward and peering at me like I was a specimen under a microscope. "Have you got any leads yet? We spoke to Karl and Monroe earlier and they wouldn't tell us anything, but we have a right to know. This is our town, and someone's going around killing strangers right under our noses."

"I'm not afraid of them," declared Mary, tapping the pavement with her stick and squaring her diminutive shoulders. She spun to me and asked, "What are you doing here anyway? Shouldn't you have left now you've had your party?"

"We just had lunch, then decided to come back into town for a walk around. We're here for another day." Arnold coughed into his fist, Mary scowled, and I noted the look they exchanged. "Problem?"

"Of course there's a problem," sighed Arnold. "Ever since you arrived there's been nothing but trouble." His pinched features contracted, forcing his cheekbones to protrude sharply, his discoloured teeth only partially hidden by mean lips. "First that mystery woman tying up the vicar and getting herself killed, then this Hayley woman, who was apparently an acquaintance of Min's. You've brought nothing but trouble to our peaceful little town."

"We don't like trouble," agreed Mary. "And you have it in spades. Come on, Arnold, we have shopping to do."

With curt nods from both, they turned and headed down the high street, bickering as they went about whether to have pork chops or lamb for their dinner.

"What a weird pair," said Dad. "He's fifty and lives with his mum."

Mum jabbed him in the ribs and said, "Don't be so quick to judge. Maybe he just loves his mum, or maybe he's had a family and his wife died, or maybe he got divorced and has no money. You don't know his story."

"You're right, love, and I apologise."

Mum beamed at him. "I forgive you."

"That's very understanding, Mum. Well done!"

"Yes, very kind," agreed Min.

"You alright, Jill?" asked Uncle Ernie, removing his hat and scratching his head in his usual manner, utterly bewildered by Mum's thoughtfulness.

"Fine," she trilled. "Mind you, he looked like a right weirdo with those sad old trousers. And who wears a parka on the hottest day of the year? Proper mad!" Mum smiled merrily, licked her lips, and asked, "Anyone fancy a drink?"

"Watch it, Mum, or you'll turn into an alcoholic. You drank loads last night."

"That was a party! I meant just a nice afternoon glass of wine to settle our nerves."

"Are we feeling nervous?" asked Dad.

"We should be. Max still hasn't caught the killer, and it's after lunchtime. Very lax."

"I'm doing my best, but to be fair this isn't easy to solve. We need to talk to the detectives."

"Then to The King's Head it is!" declared Mum. "I bet they're there. Everyone seems to spend an awful lot of time at the boozer. It's Sunday, too, so I bet the locals are having an afternoon drink after a Sunday roast on such a lovely day."

"You're right," I agreed, "that probably is the best option. To the pub it is then."

"I'm buying," said Uncle Ernie. "Everyone else has spent a fortune for the party, so it's only fair."

Nobody argued, so we headed to the pub, everyone looking forward to a cool drink as standing on the pavement in the blistering sun had left us sweaty and gasping.

Unsurprisingly, Mum was right and this was definitely where the action was. Not as busy as yesterday, the beer garden was still crowded with most picnic benches taken, and even more people lazing around on the freshly mown grass. The pub had even laid out blankets for customers who were making the most of the weather and sunning themselves, the whole vibe very laid back.

There was no sign of the crime scene tape, or any hint as to what had happened the day before, and I wondered what they'd done with Hayley's body. Would she be shipped back to her home town, collected by a funeral director, or was she still in the morgue waiting to be examined? That was an unfortunate must-do when it came to murder, although it was obvious what had killed her.

Uncle Ernie and Dad went off to get drinks, so we nabbed a table and settled, then I poured water for Anxious into the handy collapsible bowl that had been a lifesaver on many occasions, and he drank greedily before going for a wander. I prayed he didn't find another body; we had enough to deal with already.

Knowing why we were here, we each scanned the beer garden for anyone we knew, and I spotted several familiar faces. Who to talk to first? I took my chance when Phil rose from a table and headed towards the pub, leaving Swede from the camping shop sipping on the dregs of his pint. I told Mum and Min I'd be back soon, then hurried over to intercept him.

"Phil, hi. Mind if I have a word?"

"Sure. Max, isn't it?" Phil glanced back at Swede and I turned to see him hurriedly look away and stare into his pint glass.

"Yes, everything alright?"

"Sure. You?"

"Yes, all good. About yesterday, and the killing here. What did the police say?"

"That it was another poker. Like I said, it was one of mine, and I sold a load yesterday and even this morning, but I had to get away. Too much talk of murder. Not that you can get away from it here. It's all anyone is talking about."

"I bet. We bumped into Mary and her son earlier. Nobody's said much about him."

"It's not a secret. His wife left a few years ago, and as Mary is getting on he decided to move back in with her. It was a nasty divorce and he lost everything as she pushed for mistreatment or something like that. Said he was a bully and there might have been hints of abuse. It was nonsense, as Arnold wouldn't hurt a fly. Everyone knows him around here. A nice guy, if a little odd."

"That doesn't sound good. And what's with her stick?" I laughed. "She kept trying to whack everyone. She's got some strength, though, doesn't she?"

"She sure does. Mary likes to play the defenceless little old lady card, but she'd whip most of our hides. When I sold her the walking stick I told her to have a slim, lightweight one, but she wanted something weighty. If anyone's the abuser in that family," he confided, moving close and lowering his voice, "it's her." Phil laughed, then added, "Only teasing. Mary's a great character, and once you get to know her ways she's actually fun. She's always in the shop, but has been getting more forgetful."

"Have you heard any gossip about what happened? Who people think might have done it, or why?"

"Max, there is no end of gossip, but that's all it is. Nobody has any idea who it was or why they did it. We still don't even know who that other dead woman was."

"Has her photo been shown to everyone?"

"No idea, mate. I'm not a copper. You'd have to ask them."

"I think I will. Thanks, Phil, and sorry to bother you."

"No bother, mate. It already feels like you're one of our own. I know some will give you that small town nonsense about outsiders not being welcome, but we aren't like that. If anything, we welcome new people into the area. There isn't much for the youngsters regards jobs, so they're always leaving. Some new blood is what we need."

"I feel like we've been here for years," I admitted. "It's a special town and the campsite is incredible."

"It is. A true hidden gem. Watch out for the son, though. He's bad news."

I was instantly intrigued. "How so?"

"Just rumours mostly, but I dealt with him a lot over the years. He was always up to no good, and got into trouble all the time. Carl and Maureen are great people, and so kindhearted, but nothing was ever good enough for Frankie."

"They seem like a really happy family. Sad to leave, but looking forward to spending time with their son and the grandkids."

"Sure they are, and Frankie's mellowed over the years. Once he moved away and got married, he was always a lot calmer when he visited. But you saw the state of the campsite. He never came back to help, or offer to get people in to work on the place, and Carl and Maureen weren't up to it these last few years."

"But they could have found someone. If Frankie lives hours away, it's understandable he couldn't help. He has his own business to run, doesn't he?"

"Sure, but it's not a big business like he makes out. He has a couple of removal vans and a few guys. Problem is, he likes to talk but doesn't do his fair share. He's always been work shy. Shake his hand, then you'll see what I mean."

"No callouses. Soft skin, and a weak handshake."

"Exactly! Look, I don't like to talk bad of people, but I never trusted Frankie. He'd always try to pull a fast one when he came to buy stuff from the shop. Always angling to get a discount. Everyone said the same. He's money obsessed."

"He's not getting the money from the sale of the campsite, is he?"

"No way. I spoke to Carl and Maureen recently and they know the score. The money is to go into a trust for the great-grandchildren for when they're older. If anything happens to them, he still won't get a penny. He has his own house, and the business, and if he wants more money he should buck up his ideas and actually work for it. Right, that's enough gossip from me. Time for a pint."

"Thanks for the information. See you around."

"Sure."

Phil had left me with plenty to think about, including him. Suspects seemed to be mounting, with more crawling out of the woodwork. The campsite owners' son was not as he seemed, Mary had a son, and Phil himself had an actual motive, although murder to sell pokers was rather tenuous. At this rate, I'd be suspecting the vicar. Maybe she tied herself up after killing the mystery woman. Or maybe the cops were in on it, as why hadn't the dead woman's photo been shown to everyone? And how did this link back to Hayley?

"Alright, Son?" asked Dad, weighed down by a tray of drinks like Uncle Ernie.

"Blimey, how many did you get?"

"Figured I'd get everyone two in while we were there. The bar's really busy and it's crazy hot in there. I felt like a pig in a blanket."

"Wrapped in bacon?"

"No, a jumper."

"Um, okay. And yes, I'm fine. I'll fill you in back at the picnic bench."

Ernie led the way with the other tray of booze, and once we were settled I explained what Phil had told me, but all it led to was conjecture and whispers so we wouldn't be overheard. After I'd finished my first drink and not fancying a warm second, the same as everyone else, which meant Dad had to go and buy more as Uncle Ernie had told him not to be daft and get so many, I spied the vicar so Min and I went over to have a chat. She was sitting alone on a bench by the stream, before the ground dropped to the water and the scene of the crime yesterday, so we approached and I cleared my throat.

Natasha looked up from the tablet she was writing on with a special pen, and smiled. "Hello. Nice to see you both again."

Anxious barked, making his ears bounce.

"He doesn't like being left out," I laughed.

Natasha giggled, her cheeks going rosy, and told Anxious, "And it's wonderful to see you, my new friend." She patted her lap and Anxious jumped right up then snuggled down and groaned.

"He really likes you."

"We all do," said Min. "How are you doing after yesterday? It must have been so scary, but you handled it really well."

"Oh, I'm fine. Nothing much fazes me. Yes, it was rather unsettling, but I was worried about that poor woman more than anything. Nobody knows who she was yet, which is most disturbing. Did you have a nice party?"

"The party was great," I said. "We had a lovely time meeting some old friends. Natasha, have you got any new insights into what might be behind this? I assume you know what happened to Hayley? You were here, right?"

"I was. A terrible business. Whoever is doing this must be very disturbed. I feel sorry for them. They must be in an awful state."

"They must," Min agreed. "Are there any locals who have issues that might have gotten out of hand and caused them to act this way?"

"Gosh, no. Nobody that I know of. Everyone's very friendly around here."

"Ask her," said Min.

"Ask what?"

"About the shoes."

"What about the shoes?" I wondered, not understanding.

"Then I'll do it." Min turned back to Natasha and asked, "Do you know if any babies ever went missing? Probably a few years ago. Up at the campsite possibly? Maybe someone's child got taken, or maybe someone's baby died."

"Min, what's got into you? Why are you thinking like this? We found a pair of red baby shoes, that's all. You're going to a very dark place here."

"Actually, that sounds kind of familiar," said Natasha, rubbing her nose and losing her focus as she tried to remember.

"See?" gloated Min.

"Yes, a long time ago, a couple were staying at the campsite with their young son and he went missing. He must have only been one or something. Half the village went up there looking for him, and he was found in the end. Just wandered off. There was a concern he'd got lost in the woods, or even drowned in the lake, or at that age he could have drowned in the stream. It was a very upsetting few hours, but he was found safe and sound in the end."

"That's good news," I said, frowning at Min.

"Yes. Sorry to ask, but the shoes were bugging me. I wonder why they were left there?"

"I'm afraid I have no idea, my dear."

I turned at the sound of Dad calling me, so made my excuses and left after Min said she'd stay for a minute to carry on chatting.

Chapter 16

"Was the vicar any help?" asked Dad as he handed out the drinks.

"Thanks. Not really, no. She's a nice woman, and handling it well, but the only thing she helped with was this obsession Min has with a pair of old baby shoes we found in the woods earlier."

"What baby shoes?" squealed Mum. "You never mentioned anything about shoes."

"Mum, it's no big deal. But Min got rather obsessed when we found them, then asked Natasha about them. She said a few years back a child went missing, but he was found. I'm guessing they were his."

"That doesn't sound right to me." Mum frowned, then nudged Dad.

"Eh? Love, I'm not sure what you expect me to say."

"To back me up!"

"Okay. Yes, your mother's right. That sounds very suspicious."

"Mum, why doesn't it sound right?"

"Because you don't leave baby shoes behind, and you don't lose them. Where did you find them?"

"In a striped bag hanging from a tree. I assume someone found the bag and hung it up."

"Nobody does that!" Mum glared, daring me to argue.

"Then why were they there?"

"Don't get smart with me. You're not too old for me to put you over my knee and give you a right spanking."

Holding back my laughter, I told her, "One, I'd flatten you as I weigh over double what you do. Two, I definitely am way too old. And three, you or Dad never laid a finger on me."

"He was always such a good boy," Mum told Dad, sighing.

"He sure was. A delight. Same as now."

Both looked at me with the love I knew they felt and I felt in return, but it was clear Mum had a thing about these shoes just like Min. Feeling rather foolish, I removed them from my satchel and placed the bag on the table.

"Is that the bag?" asked Mum.

"Yes. I don't even know why I took it, and I'm sure it means nothing. Weird, but I felt compelled to bring it with me."

"Weirdo," noted Dad helpfully.

"You guys need to chill," said Uncle Ernie. "You think everything is a clue."

"Sometimes they are," countered Mum expertly.

"And sometimes things are exactly what they appear to be. You should take a step back."

"You're right. I don't know what came over me."

"Men!" shouted Mum, throwing her arms up and ignoring the looks from the other customers. "You don't understand at all. Of course you took them. It's like the saddest sight in the world." Mum picked up the dainty red leather shoes, studied them, laid them down, then sobbed. Dad put his arm around her and met my and his brother's eyes with a shrug.

"What's wrong, Mum?"

"Don't you understand? The only reason these shoes were in the woods is because a baby died."

"You don't know that," said Uncle Ernie, daring to defy her but ducking as she glanced up for fear of *the glare*.

"I do. It's a memorial. Is that the right word? An offering maybe, like some cultures make to their dead. A parent of a child who died put those shoes on the tree because they lost their beautiful baby. I bet they were never even worn and they bought them because they were cute, but the poor little thing never even got to wear them."

Dad picked them up and studied them, then nodded. "She's probably right. There isn't even a scuff on them. The weather has got to them and the laces are quite brittle, but the leather is still decent. Probably put them there when the cute things were brand new." Dad placed the shoes back on the table and we stared at them, wondering what, if anything, this might mean regards our case.

"Where did you get those from?" asked Phil as he passed by on the way to the bar yet again.

"The shoes?"

"Yeah." Phil scratched his head, frowning, then said, "I'm positive I've seen them before. Must be one of the grandkids' old ones. Maybe. Not sure. Weird you've got them on the table."

"I found them up at the campsite."

"Oh, right! Just some lost property, eh?" Phil wandered off, still scratching his head, muttering to himself about oddball out-of-towners.

"Now that was suspicious," noted Dad with a wink for me.

"Or he thought he recognised them and thinks we're nutters for having random shoes on a picnic bench. Guys, I think we need to lighten up. I'll put them away before we get chucked out or hauled off to the local clinic for a head inspection." As I was about to do so, Min returned and her eyes widened.

"You brought them here? Why?"

"No idea. I was just telling the others that I don't know why I picked them up. You were convinced they were so important and I didn't want to leave them behind. It was irrational, but something made me do it."

"And I was telling everyone," said Mum, "that the only reason they were in the woods is if a baby died. They're a memorial, or an offering. Something like that."

"An offering to a dead child," murmured Min, sniffling back the tears.

Uncle Ernie cleared his throat and told everyone, "That's enough. You are all in way too deep with this mystery stuff and trying to find meaning in things that don't have any. Someone lost a pair of shoes. End of."

"Maybe he's right," admitted Min. "Oh, is that for me?" She nodded to the full glass of wine.

"Sure it is, love," said Dad. "My treat. Drink up, as we've almost finished ours."

"Yes, and no more," I told him. "It's the afternoon, and you'll be sloshed by evening otherwise."

"So what? We're on holiday," he protested.

"You'll be getting a big tummy," I teased, knowing how much he'd hate that, and how much Mum would too.

"Then he's definitely had enough." Mum snatched his almost finished cider, but he was having none of it and took it back then drank with gusto before she could try again.

"Ah, so good. Right, what's next? We need to crack on with this before the trail goes cold."

"How about talking to the detectives? Oh, and there's Swede from the camping shop. I already spoke to him, but now he's alone as Phil just left, so maybe it's worth asking him about everyone in case something else comes up."

"We'll do it," declared Mum. "Better to have someone new talk to him. Jack and Ernie can come with me, but I'll do the talking."

"Don't you always," muttered Dad, then grabbed for his drink to hide behind and pretend he hadn't spoken, forgetting it was empty.

"What exactly does that mean, Jack Effort? Are you saying I'm a jabbermouth?"

"Um, no," he ventured.

"Oh, so I'm a weak-willed, subservient woman who knows her place and should never speak up, is that it?" she demanded.

"Course not, love," spluttered Dad, having snatched Uncle Ernie's pint.

"Good." Mum kissed Dad's cheek, winked at me, and told Min, "I love him really. Just my little game."

"You were very convincing," stammered Min.

"Because I wasn't joking." Mum glared at Min, Min ducked and sipped her wine, then Mum burst out laughing and said, "Sorry, I shouldn't tease like that."

"No, you shouldn't, Mum. Especially not to Min. You scared her."

"I wasn't scared. I know Jill loves Jack as much as I love you."

"Aw, aren't they so sweet?" cooed Mum. "Come on, everyone, let's get cracking." Mum stood, so Dad and Ernie followed in her wake, her swishing wide-hemmed dress, not to mention the colour and her general appearance, meaning there was plenty of space around her.

Min sat, and Anxious hopped up onto the bench beside her. I rubbed his head as I asked, "How did it go with the vicar? Anything of help?"

"No, I was just chatting." Min had a faraway look in her eyes and was smirking, so there was clearly something up.

"What's going on?"

"Nothing. Why do you ask?" She turned her head away and I heard a little giggle, but then she turned back, smiled, and reached out to take my hand.

"Because you seem awfully chipper."

"Chipper? Since when does anyone say that?"

"Since now?"

Min giggled again and shook her head. "You are one adorable but slightly eccentric man, Max Effort."

"And you are one adorable, but definitely bonkers, lady, Min Effort."

"Then we can be mad together! Let's go have a word with the detectives. And isn't it weird around here? Everyone seems to spend their life at this pub. Oh, Natasha is holding a kind of memorial at the church later. A way to show our respects for the deceased. We should go."

"Of course. That's very kind of her. I guess it is a little strange here, but it's a beautiful weekend, so I doubt it's always like this. I'm sure it's because of the murders. Everyone wants to gossip. It makes it easier for us though. Rather than traipsing around the town, most people we want to talk to are in one place. I know there are lots of other shops, and people we could question, but we can't interrogate the entire population. I'm not even sure who else we should be talking to."

"Me either. It could be anyone, or nobody who even lives here. If it's a stranger to everyone, then we'll never figure it out."

"Oh, I'm sure we will," I replied, getting that familiar tingle at the back of my neck and a hint of an as yet unformed thought niggling away that told me we were getting close but still had a ways to go yet.

"Do you know something?" Min tugged at my vest, eyes wide, a grin spreading. "You do, don't you?"

"Nothing yet, but I'm getting that feeling. I'm sure that if we keep pursuing this, we'll figure it out. Actually, I'm positive."

"My hero." Min pecked my cheek, looking super proud. I couldn't help smiling at her optimism.

"Let's ask the detectives a few questions and take it from there, shall we?"

"Sure. Let's do it."

Anxious had another drink, then I stowed the bowl in my satchel along with the shoes and other random things I always carried since I got my vanlife feet, and we wandered over to Karl and Monroe, both men looking strange to me because they were out of their magician clothes. They looked much more normal now they wore jeans and lightweight shirts, each with a pair of dark shades, giving off an unmistakable cop vibe.

As they were alone, I thought it would be okay to say hello, so did exactly that. Both men turned as one, nodded, then greeted us in a friendly enough manner, but there was clearly something going on as they weren't as jovial as they had been and there were no handshakes.

"Everything okay?" asked Min. "You seem rather off. Was it a heavy night of drinking, or is it work?"

Karl said, "We never drink to excess, especially when there's a murder to solve. In case you were wondering, the beers are alcohol free, and were yesterday. We take our work very seriously."

Monroe added, "But we have no issue with you guys. We're just frazzled after a long evening of paperwork on a Saturday night, which our wives weren't best pleased about. We're never out late on the weekends."

"Or in the week," laughed Karl. "In case you hadn't noticed, this is usually a very quiet place. It suits us perfectly."

"You both live here?" I asked.

"Sure," said Karl. "We cover a large area, but we live locally. It's why we got the case. What gives? What are you two up to?"

Min glanced at me and I nodded, knowing she was keen to take more of a lead in this latest murder mystery and to not feel like I was taking control. I was happy to let her ask the questions. "We aren't up to anything. We just wanted to have a word to see if you have any progress. Anything that you think might lead somewhere. We also wanted to ask why the mystery woman's photo hasn't been shown to people. Is there a reason?"

Now it was Karl and Monroe's turn to glance at each other and for Monroe to nod to his partner that he should answer. Karl took a deep breath as if to calm himself before dealing with us, then said, "We have no real leads at all. Natasha Green, our lovely vicar, has been a great help, but it hasn't got us any further on in the investigation. She's the one who dealt with the woman the most besides you two, and we've already spoken to you. As far as we can fathom, there is no link between the two deceased, although that doesn't mean there isn't one. Our other options are that we're dealing with someone who merely got a taste for killing and decided that Hayley was an easy mark." Karl shrugged; that was everything they had.

"And the photo?" asked Min. "Why not show it to everyone? They might recognise her."

"We've shown a photo to a few people, those who we believe might have seen our mystery woman, but they're under strict instructions not to talk about it with anyone. Including you pair."

"Why?" I couldn't help asking. "Surely it's better for everyone to see."

"Guys," said Monroe, "that's not how these things work. We need to keep this quiet and on a low profile, then it goes through the appropriate channels, and if we don't come up with anything, then more information, including a photo of the deceased, can be released to the public. But only as a last resort. The answer to why that's the case is because the only images we have of her are ones where she's looking absolutely terrified and is most definitely dead. That's not the kind of thing you go showing regular folk. We can't be traumatising people. Not to mention the fact that it would be awful for her family if they found out she was dead by seeing a photo of her on national TV. We don't roll that way. Does that help you to understand?"

"Of course! We hadn't thought of it like that," said Min, looking relieved and smiling despite the grim topic.

"We do know what we're doing," laughed Karl. "Now, it's your turn to share. What have you unearthed? Anything we should know about?"

"What do you know about the campsite owners' son?" asked Min. "We thought he was a decent guy but heard a few things about him. And he was skulking around in the middle of the night at the house. Should we be concerned?"

Karl and Monroe hissed and their jaws clenched. Monroe told us, "Frankie's not the greatest. Got into a bit of bother over the years with the local cops, but nothing more than a little tomfoolery when he was young. But he has a reputation as being a chancer and very workshy. His folks set him up with the removal business years ago when he moved away and found it hard to cope, but by all accounts he's doing okay. Although not as well as he could if he actually put the hours in. Nothing sinister, though, and he knows the score regards the campsite and his parents money and that he won't see a penny of it. He likes to pretend otherwise to save face, but everyone knows the truth. There was bad blood for a while because of it, but he has a house and business and they don't trust him not to squander it so it goes to his grandkids once Carl and Maureen are gone."

"That's what we heard," I told them. "He isn't a suspect?"

"Frankie?" asked Monroe, almost choking on his alcohol-free beer. "He's too lazy to be bothered going around murdering people, and he hasn't got the smarts to do it and not be seen. He wasn't around yesterday here when Hayley was killed, that much we do know. Have you seen the size of him? No way he wouldn't have been spotted."

"What about Phil?" asked Min. "He's selling a lot of pokers."

"Now you really are clutching at straws! Phil's a good guy and there's zero chance it was him. He was in plain sight when Hayley was murdered."

"No, he wasn't," I told them. "He was around after, but not when she was killed."

"I get your point, but again, he's not on our list of suspects."

"Then who is?" asked Min, stepping close to hear the juicy answer.

"Nobody," admitted Monroe with a frown. "It's got us stumped so far. Look, if there's anything at all that you've seen or heard that seems iffy, no matter how inconsequential it might seem, then now is the time to tell us. This has already gone on too long without us uncovering anything, so spill it if you have something to say."

Min and I stared at my satchel, then I nodded and pulled out the striped bag and opened it for them to see inside.

"Baby shoes?" asked Karl with a shake of his head. "I don't understand."

"Natasha said that a few years ago a young child got lost up at the campsite, but then was found. Maybe these could be the child's?"

"Maybe."

"Could it mean something?"

"I don't see how," said Karl. "Where exactly did you find them?"

"Hanging from a tree. I took them, but I'm not sure why. How old do you think they are?"

Karl peered into the bag then pulled one out by a lace and inspected it. "At least ten years is my guess. The bag is almost rotten and I think I recognise it. We used to have one. The shoes are from a local company that went out of business about eight years ago, so they are at least that old."

"So, they are local shoes?" asked Min.

"For sure. So most likely they're from one of the residents. Probably lost them and someone hung them up."

"But what would someone be doing with shoes for a toddler up in the woods?" asked Min.

"Who knows? Okay, thanks for telling us, but I think you're on the wrong track here. Stuff gets lost all the time, and these are ancient. Nothing to do with our inquiry."

I replaced the bag in my satchel, we thanked them for their time, then returned to find Mum, Dad, and Uncle Ernie grinning from ear to ear.

Chapter 17

"What are you looking so pleased about? Have you cracked the case wide open?"

"Maybe we have," said Mum smugly.

"Could be," agreed Dad.

"We might know something that could help," said Uncle Ernie, playing it safe as he clearly wasn't as convinced as them.

"Then spill it, as the detectives don't have anything yet and the trail is most definitely going cold if not freezing," I said.

Dad opened his mouth to speak, but Mum slapped her palm over his face and growled, "I'm telling this, not you. You'll only get things muddled up."

Dad nodded, so Mum removed her hand, and he said, "Suit yourself, but make sure you tell it properly."

I sighed. "Guys, just tell us. And don't turn it into a long, drawn-out story either."

"Since when have I ever done that?" Mum pouted, ignoring the sniggering from the rest of us.

"Never," I said, poker-faced.

"Exactly. Now, where was I? Oh yes, so, that Swede is a nice man, very friendly, and I think he's a bit of a gossip." Again, she ignored the sniggers. "He told us some interesting facts about a few people, but most notably about the actual detectives."

"Most notably?" I asked, eyebrow raised. "Training to be a detective yourself, are you?"

"Stop interrupting! Yes, Swede told us that Karl has, or maybe had, a thing for the vicar. That they dated and it was going well, but then she called it off. Apparently, they were set to be engaged."

"Nobody ever mentioned that before," said Min, eyes gleaming.

"Right?" said Mum. "It didn't end well and he wasn't happy about it, moping around for weeks, and even kept interrupting her sermons. Once he turned up at a wedding she was performing and ruined the whole day. Natasha exploded and told him in front of loads of people that it was over. Can you imagine?"

"She doesn't seem the type to do that unless she had very good reason," I said.

"And she's a vicar, so she has to try to stay calm and set a good example. Well, after the dust settled, things were rather frosty, but not so long ago Karl tried again to get back with her, saying he couldn't live without her."

"Mum, are you sure about this? It doesn't sound like how either of them would act."

"We heard it too," said Uncle Ernie.

"So I'm not making any of this up. Max, that's fishy, right?"

"I'm not sure. It's odd Natasha didn't mention it, but then again, why would she? She's not going to think he murdered people."

"But here's where it gets really juicy. Apparently, a local woman said that Karl tried to force her to pretend to be his girlfriend, that he insinuated that if she didn't play along he'd make sure she got parking tickets and wouldn't leave her alone until she did what he asked. He wanted to make Natasha jealous. She was scared, so went along with it at first, then told him where to shove it and reported him. Of course, she didn't get parking tickets as then it would be obvious she was telling the truth, and nobody believed her, but the rumours still spread."

"That's crazy. A detective can't act like that," gasped Min.

"So are you saying Swede thinks Karl murdered the women? Why?"

"He didn't say that. He was just gossiping. But it got us to thinking. Maybe he arrested this woman that impersonated Natasha, or maybe he knew her from another town, and wanted to mess with the vicar by getting his friend to impersonate her and ruin things. It's possible, right?"

"I guess. Well done, Mum, and you two. It's certainly put things in a whole new light. But we can't go accusing detectives of double murder unless we have a very solid case."

"The man sounds like bad news, if it's true, but murder? No way." Uncle Ernie shook his head, looking each of us in the eye. "Right?"

We agreed that it was very unlikely it was Karl, but it would make us more cautious going forward about what information we shared, and to possibly speak to Natasha about it soon too.

"Did he say anything else?"

"Just gossip about the woman whose poker was used, or that she says was stolen. Apparently, her son was married for a few years, but everyone reckons he was making it up as nobody met her. He left the town, lived away for a while, was supposed to have been married with a child even though he's getting on, then came back with his tail between his legs. Nobody ever saw the wife or the child though. All pretty weird stuff about local crazies."

"He certainly seemed a little strange. Anything else?" I asked, wondering how much of the gossip was actually true and how much was utterly made up by busybodies.

"Yes, quite a bit actually. Swede loves to gossip and he told us that the campsite owners' son is trouble. That he got into bother when he was younger and his parents had to keep bailing him out. That nobody around here trusted him and he was really bitter about not inheriting anything from them. They set him up in business, but the money from the sale of the campsite will go into trust for his grandchildren."

"We already knew that. We told you, remember?"

"Yes, but not all of that. And there were a few things about Phil too. Swede said he likes Phil and they usually have a few pints together on the weekends, but what he let slip was very interesting."

"Blimey, Mum, how much did this guy tell you?"

"Loads!" Mum grinned, looked forlornly at her empty glass, then said, "Phil once got arrested for hitting a customer with a poker. Apparently, it happened a few times, but this time the guy wanted to press charges so he was arrested. Eventually, the man changed his mind and Phil was let off, but he's got a temper. He used to get into brawls all the time, but he's been much better lately."

"So what we're saying is that it could have been almost everyone we've met, including the ones in charge of the case?" I sighed, the beginnings of a migraine coming on."

"Pretty much sums it up, Son," laughed Dad. "Come on, let's get out of here. If we stay any longer, we'll be wanting another drink."

We agreed, so left rather reluctantly, as despite the weird information we'd gleaned, it really was a lovely beer garden and the drinks were both delicious and affordable.

Chapter 18

When we arrived back at the campsite and I parked up and everyone left, Min dashed outside, closely followed by me and Anxious. The three of us stood back and admired Vee, a sigh escaping our lips.

"Oh, isn't she wonderful? It's so great to be back home. I missed her even though we've been driving around."

"I know exactly what you mean. Seeing her in a field with the gazebo beside her is where she belongs. Where we all belong."

Min and I linked arms, Anxious sat between us, and I felt as happy as I'd ever felt. Vee gleamed in the dappled light, her two-tone orange and white paint job still fresh. It was different now because of Min's rather unconventional and prolonged marriage proposal sprayed onto the lower panels, but if anything it made the old girl more part of us. More a member of the family.

For no other reason than because we wanted to, we went inside and sat on the bench seat, studying the interior and appreciating the workmanship that had gone into the cupboards, the counter housing sink and hob, and even the old-fashioned and often annoying huge gearstick and basic dashboard. I loved it, maybe more than I should have, but it was home and that's where the heart is no matter whether it comprises bricks and mortar, or a vehicle older than my parents.

"What shall we do for the rest of the day?" asked Min.

"Solve a murder?" I grinned, then winked, and Min's expression changed from smiling to wide-eyed.

"You know who did it, don't you? Max, how could you!?" Min batted at my arm playfully, shaking her head in wonder.

"Hey, it isn't my fault. After all the gossip this afternoon, I figured it was a lost cause, but on the drive home everything suddenly clicked into place. I need to think things through more, come up with a plan, but I'm sure I at least know who did it, if not exactly why yet. Do you mind if I pull out the bed and lie down for a while so I can mull this over?"

"Of course not. Can we stay too?"

"I think you know the answer to that." I kissed Min, ruffled Anxious' head, then Min scooped him up while I sorted out the rock n roll bed before we lay back, Anxious between us, and Min left me to my thoughts.

Soon, I was in that peculiar zone that only happens during summer when the air is hot and still and all feels at peace in the world. Time loses meaning, everything else fades away, and all that remains is the heat, the birds chattering in the trees, bees buzzing in and out through the windows and doors, and the occasional breeze carrying scents of surrounding farms and the sweet perfume of flowers.

I was neither awake nor asleep, everything hazy with thoughts left to roam. Not pushing anything, just watching as they drifted by and slowly things came together, in no small part thanks to Min and Anxious being beside me and supporting our family in any way they could.

We must have lay like that for at least an hour, and when I stirred I knew they were both asleep by their breathing. Carefully, I slipped off the end of the bed, went outside, and stretched out my arms, lifting my face to the sun poking through between the trees. What a beautiful way to live this was. But the longer I stood there, the more I realised that it went beyond the travelling and the new faces I met along the way. It was more about the lifestyle it forced upon you. The fact that whenever possible, come sun or come rain, you had to spend most of your time outdoors. That was the true draw of the lifestyle I had chosen.

Maybe that could work in a different way?

Mind made up, and certain it was what Min wanted, I made a phone call. Once that was done, I made a few other calls, sorted a few things out in the gazebo, then made a mental checklist of what was available for dinner. I settled on an old favourite, then prepped that and stowed it in Tupperware so I could quickly get the meal bubbling away later on. Drained by the heat, I simply sat in my camping chair and enjoyed the solitude.

I assumed that my folks and Uncle Ernie were having an afternoon siesta, too, as nobody was around and everyone was quiet. If Mum and Dad were awake, there would be noise; that was how they rolled and always had. You wouldn't find them sitting quietly and reading, or just soaking up the atmosphere. They would rather chat, or shout, enjoying each other's company as much now as when they'd first got together.

Min and I were different, yet the love was the same. We were happy with the silence and could sit for hours without saying a word, reading books, or more often than not just relaxing. But this time to myself was also precious, and I never minded being alone. Even though occasionally vanlife got rather lonely, I even revelled in that as it brought home how amazing life was and how fortunate I was to be able to afford this strange, nomadic existence I'd chosen for myself.

I tried to come up with a plan that would see this finished with, but it eluded me. Was there a way to get an admission and for justice to be served without it becoming convoluted and dangerous? How best to approach this without anyone being put at risk? Various scenarios played out in my head, but none of them felt right. There was something missing and I couldn't put my finger on what it was. As was always the case, I knew better than to push things, so emptied my mind and merely sat and watched the world go by.

Which meant I watched absolutely nothing as there was no activity at this closed campsite apart from our small party and everyone but me was fast asleep. I wondered how often you had to cut the grass and how much a new ride-on mower would cost. How did you do the mowing if the place was full of guests? I supposed you had to wait until people left and do a patch at a time, but that didn't seem like a very sensible way of doing things. I'd never considered the day-to day work of running a campsite before, but now I began to ponder such things I realised there was no end of other duties that had to be performed.

Emptying bins, cleaning toilets and shower stalls. Ensuring there was loo roll and soap and what about the washing up area? You'd have to give them a clean a few times a day, I assumed, and you'd also need a system for recycling and bin collections, and what if you wanted to go off for a few days? You couldn't, could you? You'd be tied to the campsite dealing with customers coming and going every day, and have to be available to deal with any queries or problems. Would you offer facilities for people to empty their toilets? That'd be a hassle, wouldn't it? How did such things function? I had no idea.

You'd need staff to cover for you if you went away, or you'd never get a break. Gosh, it wasn't as simple as you'd think, and I was sure I was missing most of what went on. Still, it would beat working for a living, not that I had to do that because of the rental income and the nice nest egg I'd added to over the years, even though everything had been split fifty-fifty with Min when we divorced. The one thing we'd both always been good at was being careful with our cash.

Neither of us were big spenders, and had always valued our money and made sure to save whenever we could. You never knew what the future would bring, so it was always best to be prepared, and who could have seen me becoming a vanlifer coming? I certainly had never even thought about it before I suddenly decided to change my life entirely and roam the country uncovering beautiful countryside and seemingly no end of mysteries I somehow became embroiled in.

My musings ended up getting me worried. Would we run out of money? Was life about to throw us a zinger and our happiness be ruined? Why would it be? Because my life seemed to consist of endless drama of one sort or another. Interspersed with the quiet times were these mad happenings that I never anticipated. No way! I could handle whatever life threw at me, I was sure, so why worry about what hadn't even happened yet? That was no way to live. You never knew with any certainty what was next, so the only thing to do was enjoy the moment and let the cards fall where they may.

Calmed by my own personal telling off, I relaxed again and let it all pass me by without dwelling on any single thought. As I zoned-out and stared off into space, the sun warm on my skin, I was almost overwhelmed with a sudden and deeply intense feeling of happiness in a way I'd never experienced before. Right here, right now, there were no problems. Everything was perfect. This moment was precious, priceless even, and I stayed in this peculiar moment of now for the longest time. Even after I emerged from it, I felt the peace remain. The happiness and contentment with my life and the world around me, and I got a new appreciation for just sitting and doing absolutely nothing at all.

Inevitably, a solution to the problem of getting justice for the deceased came to me seemingly from nowhere. I jumped up and did a little jig, then felt self-conscious as I spun in a circle and noticed Min and Anxious standing in the doorway, heads cocked to the side, watching with amused expressions.

"Hello," I laughed, "did you both have a nice nap?"

"We did. And it looks like you've been having a party without us. What are you so happy about, and why are you dancing? Um, you were dancing, weren't you? Either that, or you were having some kind of seizure."

"Hey, my dancing isn't that bad!"

"If you say so. Any chance of a coffee?"

"Sure."

Anxious jumped down and trotted over to say hello, so I gave him a fuss, then kissed Min and fixed us both a drink.

"Thanks. Hey, what time is it?"

"Just gone four. Still plenty of the afternoon left and then the evening. I've prepped dinner, so it's just a matter of putting it on low to simmer for a few hours. I might cook over the fire as then it means we haven't got to stick around and worry about gas. It's not the best idea to leave the burner on with nobody here."

"Why? Where are we going? And how did you manage to do so much? We were only asleep for a few minutes after you."

"More like an hour or so," I teased. "I thought you were never going to wake up."

"We've had a busy day, and yesterday was a late night. So, what's the plan?" Min sipped her coffee but kept her gleaming eyes on me, clearly keen to get the murders solved.

"How about we head back into town? I think I know a way of getting this done. It might not play out exactly as we want, but hopefully we'll get a confession. What do you say?"

"You're on. Are we going to take the others?"

"What do you think? No way will Mum and Dad let us go without them. They love being involved. Dad will have a field day with the wiki page and the forum and be telling everyone that he solved the crime this time. No chance of him missing an opportunity like that."

"Unless we sneak off and don't tell them." Min winked, then laughed, knowing as well as I did that we'd never hear the end of it if we tried to pull a fast one.

"Mum would disown us both."

"She would."

As we finished our coffees, Mum emerged from the bell tent, checked out the site, then spotted us and hurried over whilst waving, and shouting, "It's me, Mum," as if we'd forgotten what she looked like. Who could forget the riot of colour? As was expected, she'd changed into yet another dress. This time she fashioned a very in-your-face red number with white dots, white high heels, a white bandana, with her red hair poking through. It went without saying that her make-up was better than you'd get in John Lewis at the make-up section.

"Wait for me!" yelled Dad, then sprang from the tent, spied Mum, and raced over.

"You're both looking very smart," I noted. "Dad, you got changed too? Clean tee, polished shoes, and you've even done your hair."

"Got to make the effort, Max. Ha ha. Geddit? Make the effort, Max."

"Yes, I get it. Mum, you look lovely. Give us a twirl."

"Ooh, thanks, love." Mum beamed as she spun, her dress flaring, her bare arms flung out to the sides.

"You do look fantastic," said Min. "But why are you both so dressed up? What's the plan?"

"We assumed you pair had a plan," said Dad. "Aren't we going to catch the murderer and solve the case? I've got a good idea who it is, and I'm itching to get going. You two coming? And where's that brother of mine?" Dad turned to Uncle Ernie's tent but the door was closed.

"He's probably still sleeping," said Min.

"Sleeping!? We haven't got time for that. We need to get going. We are going out again, aren't we?"

"What makes you assume that?" I asked, acting innocent.

"Max, your mother took an age to get ready, and I've got a fresh T-shirt on and Brylcreemed my hair. We had better be going out for the evening."

"He's teasing you," said Mum. "You are, aren't you? I wouldn't want my new outfit to go to waste."

"New?" spluttered Dad. "You told me it was an old dress, and that you hadn't bought any new clothes for months. Those dresses cost a fortune as you refuse to use any other shops apart from the most expensive one."

"I told you, Mary who works there knows what I like, and they're the only place that sells dresses like this anyway."

"But it is new?"

"Not really new. More like a little bit old."

"And have you ever worn it before?" Mum mumbled something nobody could hear but everyone could guess, but Dad was having none of it. "What was that?"

"No, I haven't worn it before," admitted Mum, actually dipping her head a few millimetres.

"And when did you buy this old dress that you haven't worn before?"

"Last week." Mum brightened and added, "But Max and Min think it was worth the money, don't you?" She turned to us, eyes pleading.

"No way am I getting involved in this," I said hurriedly. "We both agree you look lovely, but the rest is down to you pair."

"See, they think it was worth the high cost."

"What high cost? How much was it?" Dad was getting a sweat on, and looked ready to cut up the credit cards.

"Not much, and stop fretting. We can afford it."

"Not now, we can't. We'll be eating old cheese and mouldy bread from a skip now. Do you want us to get food poisoning and die? You do, don't you? You made us eat mangy old cheese, and not even good Cheddar, and you'll starve and then you'll be too thin to even fit into the dress."

The temperature lowered by several degrees as Dad realised the ultimate mistake he'd made.

Mum's smile spread, the evil glee building, and she winked at us before whirling on Dad. In a low, ominous voice, she asked, "So you think I'm fat? You're saying I'm a big lump and should go on a diet of bread and cheese?" She was crowing with her victory voice, knowing no way would Dad give her grief about the cost now as he'd fallen for her cunning trap.

"I didn't say that. You look perfect, love. The dress is lovely, and your shape fits it perfectly."

"And what shape would that be? Big, fat, and lumpy shape?"

"Of course not. Hey, there's Ernie." Dad darted off, pleased to have found an excuse to escape Mum's pretend ire.

"That was mean," I laughed.

"You know your father is always like that when I buy a new dress. Sometimes I need to turn the tables on him so he backs down." Mum giggled, pleased with her ploy, then in a more serious tone asked, "Do you have a plan? Do you know who did it? Will you tell me?"

"I think it's best if I wait until later to explain anything. I don't want anyone getting wind of what we're up to."

"And what are we up to?"

"We're going to get justice for those women, and ensure that Natasha is never worried about getting tied to a chair again."

"I knew it! You do know who did it. Tell me, please?" Mum put her hands together and dipped her head.

"Sorry, but it's best I don't. Like I said, this will work better if you're in the dark."

"Do you know?" Mum asked Min.

"Not yet, no."

"Max, that is so mean. You should tell Min."

"So she'll tell you?"

"The thought never crossed my mind."

Dad and Uncle Ernie returned, so we agreed to leave in ten minutes once everyone had sorted things out.

Half an hour later and we were off, which was a miracle where Mum was concerned.

Chapter 19

"What time is the service? Did you put dinner on? Should we go back so I can change? I don't feel dressed up enough to go to church."

I glanced in the rearview mirror at everyone else squished together, then at Mum sitting beside me, and opened and closed my mouth but no words came. What could I possibly say? I decided to keep it brief, and safe. "Half five."

"So there is time to get changed?"

After a deep, calming breath, I told her, "You look great. No need to change."

"What was that?" called Dad from the rear.

"Nothing."

"Sorry?"

"I said nothing," I bellowed.

"You did. I heard you."

"Then why are you asking?" That kept him quiet, so I focused on my driving, more relaxed with the roads now we'd done the route a few times. Thankfully, we entered a lovely quiet zone for a few minutes, allowing me to gather my thoughts and think a little more about what to do once we arrived. The answer was simple. At first, I would do nothing.

"Why is the vicar holding a service again?" asked Mum, scowling at me as we hit a pothole right when she was re-applying her lipstick.

"In memory of the two murdered women. She wanted to do something to give them a send-off. Both are still in the morgue, according to the detectives, but Natasha didn't want to wait. Hayley will be taken back home tomorrow, I expect, and there will be a proper funeral there, but who knows what will happen to the other woman unless her identity is discovered. This is a way to say goodbye and to do something. I think Natasha wants it to give herself some closure more than anything, but it's a nice thought."

"Are we supposed to get up and say something?"

"Mum, it doesn't work like that. Like I said, this isn't a funeral. It's more of a memorial service."

"How is it a memorial when nobody knows who the one woman was, and nobody liked Hayley?" bellowed Dad.

"That's not the point, Dad. It's a respect thing. Natasha wants to do it, and she was the one who was assaulted, so we should support her. And actually, I think it's very kind and considerate."

"Plus, it should mean all the likely suspects are in one place, right, Son?" cackled Dad, rubbing his hands together.

"Exactly. So we don't want to miss it. Min, are you okay?"

"Fine, thanks. A bit squashed, but we're nearly there, aren't we?"

"We sure are. The high street is quiet now, so I'll park here. It will make it easy to leave later." I reversed into the spot, pleased I did it in one go, having finally mastered the esoteric art of controlling the campervan. After so many years using power steering, hauling on the large steering wheel took some getting used to, but now I was a pro and most times it didn't even bring me out in a sweat.

Everyone piled out, those in the back grateful for some room to stretch their legs, me in the front delighted to not be shouted at, Mum the happiest as she could use the mirror to finish her make-up without it being smeared all over her face. Once we'd waited a while, Dad hurried her up and she actually listened, so it was only another five minutes until she was satisfied and we could get going.

First job was a short walk for Anxious, so we followed the river upstream a little then found a delightful area by the riverbank that wasn't the pub for a change, and had a pleasant stroll while Anxious frolicked in the long grass and even went for a quick paddle.

"This whole town keeps getting better and better," said Min as we wandered away from the others, arms linked, enjoying the more subdued decibels.

"It really does. I wonder how far you can walk along the riverbank? It looks like it goes on for miles."

"One day we'll have to come again and see. It's such a lovely town, and everyone seems so nice. There are a lot of real characters. The shops are ace, too, and I bet you can find all sorts of amazing things in Phil's shop. Just not any pokers."

"Definitely no pokers. Although, they are very well made, and look so nice."

"Max!"

"Sorry," I laughed, feeling nervous about what was to come, but trying to keep the mood light. "Did you see the deli? And there's a proper local butchers and bakers, and they have a Co-op too."

"Since when did you love the Co-op?"

"Since always. It's a handy shop. The bread's always decent in a pinch, and they have everything you need without going out of town to a big supermarket."

"Yeah, right! You love a big supermarket for the basics."

"I do," I admitted, "but you can't beat small shops and this town has so many. I bet if we wandered around properly we'd find some other cool places down the side streets and alleys."

"It's definitely our kind of place. It's not too far to the beach either. I reckon it's maybe an hour and a half to the coast, and about two hours up to Shell Island, Harlech, and even less to Barmouth or Tywyn."

"And let's not forget the incredible countryside. There are hills everywhere, but really nice gentle rolling hills. Loads of walks. And all the other towns too. Church Stretton, Ludlow, Leominster, and it's only an hour to Hereford. And we both know how beautiful Shrewsbury is. One of the nicest towns I've ever been to in my life."

"Shrewsbury is the best." Min and I held each other's gaze as our smiles spread. "Gosh, we sound like estate agents trying to convince each other that Craven Oaks is the place to be."

"We do. Maybe it is?"

"What are you saying?"

"What do you want me to be saying?"

"Hey, you two ready?" asked Uncle Ernie as he approached. "The service starts in ten and we need to get there. Sorry, was I interrupting?"

"No, it's fine. We were just saying how great it is around here."

"It's one of the best areas in the country. I love it in Shropshire. Amazing walks, incredible towns, lakes, hills, forests, ancient castles, and tasty food. But you both know that as you always lived in Shropshire."

"Yes, but not this area. It's incredible, and somehow it's like nobody knows about it."

"The country's best kept secret, and that's why it's so awesome. Not too busy."

We caught up with Mum and Dad who were trying to rush ahead so they didn't miss anything, but kept getting distracted by birds or little waterfalls, then laughing as Anxious skipped around trying to catch bugs, regretting it when he did, so we linked arms and sped up so we didn't miss the service.

By the time we arrived at the church, there was a small crowd outside the gates filing in slowly, so we joined the queue and fell silent like everyone else as a sign of respect for those who had passed. I took the time to see who I recognised. Nobody yet, as I could only see a few people, but I was certain that everyone we'd met would be here somewhere.

Waiting to greet everyone at the door was Natasha, dressed rather formally with her dog collar, a pair of sensible black trousers, a simple white shirt, and holding a stack of paper. When it was our turn, her eyes lit up and she moved in close and smiled warmly.

"Thank you so much for coming, and for everything you've done."

"It was our pleasure to help," I said.

"Of course it was. How are you doing now, Natasha?" asked Min.

"Oh, don't you worry about me. I'm fine. It shook me up, and I think I was worse a few hours later when the reality of it sank in, but my main concern is for my parishioners. Those poor women are dead, and nobody seems to have any idea why, or who did it. This is the least I can do. Just a way of showing our respect. I'm surprised at the turn out though. We'll be starting soon, and it won't take long. Of course, nobody here knew them apart from you, Min, but I don't suppose you want to stand up and say anything about Hayley as you didn't get on, did you?"

Min blanched, and said hurriedly, "That wouldn't be a good idea. Of course it's awful what happened, but I couldn't stand in front of people and say things that aren't true. You don't mind?"

"Of course not. I understand completely. I'm going to keep this simple and brief, but felt it was important to do something. In fact, if I'm being honest, this is more for me and everyone else than for those unfortunate women. A way for the community to come together and hopefully find solace, but also to encourage everyone to stay positive. We will find who did this, I'm sure of it."

"Can I have a quick word in private? Just a moment?" I asked.

Natasha glanced back at the short queue behind us, then nodded. "Sure, but can't it wait until after the service?"

"I'm afraid it will be too late then."

"Then of course." Natasha led the way around the side of the church where we could talk in private, and I explained what I had in mind, much to her chagrin.

It didn't take long to talk her around, even though she was reticent to believe me at first, convinced there must be another way. I wasn't so sure, but told her I was open to suggestions, but she came up with nothing. When asked if I'd informed the police about my plan, I had to admit that I hadn't because I was too concerned about word getting out. She admitted that was probably a very good idea as everyone seemed to know everyone else's business before the words were even out of your mouth.

With a tentative plan now finalised, we hurried back to the others and the grumbling locals still waiting outside, then we entered the church and wandered down the aisle to find a seat. Although I wanted to see who was here, the only seats were quite near the back, so once everyone else was sitting down I nipped out and walked to the front slowly, glancing left then right and checking those we'd met so far were here. They were. There were also plenty of unfamiliar faces, with locals of all ages come to honour the dead, and a surprising number of children, too, very excited and being told to shush by parents who were realising this wasn't a fun outing for the kids and having second thoughts about bringing them.

I did a quick about turn, nodded to people who made eye contact, including the detectives, Karl and Monroe, who were just a few rows back from the front. Both jolted more upright as our eyes met, and I could have sworn they knew my intentions. Was I that easy to read? I hoped not, but maybe it was just my imagination. I looked away, noted others I recognised, some of whom didn't meet my eye, then returned to my seat and sat next to the aisle so I could get up easily when the time came.

The church was as quiet as a graveyard as everyone waited for the service to start, the silence only broken by Natasha's gentle footsteps as she made her way slowly to the front, nodding to people and smiling softly as she went. She took her position in the pulpit and told us that this would be a short service of only ten minutes, but that in no way lessened the depth of emotion she felt for such terrible crimes. She explained that this was not a funeral, and was more for the community to mourn the loss of two women who certainly didn't deserve such terrible deaths, then the sermon proper began.

True to her word, Natasha kept the service brief and rather generic. Everyone understood that there was little choice for her as one woman was a complete mystery, the other known only to Min, and we all knew what she felt about Hayley. There were a few sobs, and several wails from the congregation, along with boisterous chatter from the young ones asking when it was over and could they have ice-cream after, but the service went seamlessly. Natasha did an excellent job of saying kind words about the women without it seeming like she was making anything up about them.

After a prayer at the end, something that always made me feel uncomfortable but I understood that many were religious and this was a church after all, Natasha closed the book on the lectern she'd been reading from and took a moment to look out at the sea of faces.

"Please remember to take care. Be mindful of who you are talking to and where you are. Don't go anywhere alone if you can possibly help it, and keep an eye on your neighbours. This is very important until we find out who did this. Now, although this is rather unconventional, I believe someone else wants to say a few words. Max?" Natasha nodded to me, so pushing down my nerves, I stood as all faces turned to me. Never one to volunteer for public speaking, and hating the attention, I nevertheless gripped Min's hand tightly, returned her reassuring smile, then let go and stood reluctantly.

"What's this about?" demanded Phil as he sprang to his feet. "I've got things to do. A shop to run."

"The shop's closed for the day, you dolt," called Swede. "It's almost six o'clock now. You aren't going to open again."

"Yeah," shouted someone else. "You just want to go to the pub, Phil."

"What if I do? That's allowed. What's Max got to say that we haven't already heard? He's not even from around here." There were a few murmurs of agreement, and more people stood, clearly wanting to leave, but a noise from the rear made everyone turn.

Dad turned from the door, the oversized key in his hand, and waved it in the air. "Nobody's going anywhere until Max says his piece. Everyone sit down."

There was uproar. People filled the aisle, babies cried, children demanded ice-cream, vicars went unheard, and things began to get ugly as the braver amongst the crowd marched towards Dad.

Before I could retreat and help save him, Mum stormed from the pew and barred the way, leaving everyone agog as she whirled, her dress swishing and her arms raised. "Everyone sit back down and leave my Jack alone!" she bellowed. "We are in a place of worship and you're acting like awful sinners. Sit!"

So forceful was her command that several men plonked themselves down in the aisle while others took a more sensible approach and retreated to their seats. One brave soul even tried to outstare Mum and got so close I worried there might be violence, but as Mum cast her laser eyes on him he withered and darted away hurriedly before his hair caught on fire.

Nodding to Mum and Dad, I sidestepped the men on the ground and went up to the lectern as Natasha vacated it, looking very concerned for the safety of everyone and most likely thinking the same thing as me. That Dad locking the door was a terrible idea and a total fire risk.

"Um, first of all, please nobody light a match," I joked, the humour going down terribly, as all I got was a groan from Min then a reassuring wink when our eyes met.

"What's the deal, Max?" demanded Phil, still standing until Mum coughed and he turned and had to duck as her eyes settled on him.

"Yes, I'm so sorry about this, but I couldn't think of any other way to do it."

"Do what?" someone asked.

"I need the loo," said Mary, waving her walking stick at me and nearly knocking her son out cold.

"It won't take long, Mary, so please be patient with me."

"But what do you want to say?" asked Swede, checking the door, as if considering making a break for it.

"I want to reveal who the murderer is, and tell everyone what I think happened."

"You can't do that!" blurted Karl.

"You expect us to believe you've solved the case?" asked Monroe, standing beside his partner and refusing to turn to look at Mum when she coughed again. "There's not a hint of who this might have been. We still haven't even identified the first victim."

"Then let me tell you who she was," I said, my voice little more than a whisper, but the entire church fell silent in an instant and all eyes were focused on me once again. I took a breath, smiled at Anxious as he trotted down the aisle then sat beside the pulpit as if to guard me, then began.

Chapter 20

As I opened my mouth, so the distinct click of the church door being unlocked caused everyone to turn. Moose saluted from his position beside Dad, who hadn't noticed him. I couldn't even begin to imagine how he got through a locked door, but that was Moose for you—a true ninja. Dad winked, a massive grin plastered over his shiny face, pleased to have timed things perfectly. I returned the salute to Moose, then nodded back to Dad as he opened the door and two rather bewildered officers in uniform shifted about until he leaned in close and had a word with them. They glanced up at me, then stepped inside and the door was closed behind them.

"What is going on here?" demanded Karl as he and Monroe approached me. "Who called for backup?"

"I did!" shrilled Mum, standing and taking a bow, utterly oblivious to the lack of reaction from everyone else. "My Max asked me to do it so I did. Nobody leaves until the killer's revealed," she hissed dramatically, eyes flashing with excitement.

Anxious yipped his agreement, then growled as the two detectives took up position beside him. I stepped down from the pulpit, had a quiet word with them while the noise levels rose, then with a rather reticent grunt of agreement they moved to the aisle and watched over the crowd as slowly all attention was drawn back to me.

"This is dumb," shouted Swede, and stepped into the aisle. "I'm leaving."

"Nobody leaves," insisted Monroe.

"Please let Max tell us what he knows," said Natasha, wringing her hands, moving a little closer to me so people wouldn't feel so threatened.

"Why should we?" called out Mary, poking her son with her stick until he shifted into the aisle so she could get out and join him. "We're not listening to any more of this nonsense. Come on, Arnold, we're leaving."

Arnold's gaze rose until our eyes met, the fear in those brown orbs easy to read.

It was now or never, so without giving it too much thought as I worried I might freeze, I simply stated, "The woman who impersonated Natasha, and was pinned to the tree with one of Phil's pokers, was Arnold's wife." I kept my focus on him, and he blanched, then tugged nervously at the zipper of his parka. "Nobody else has ever met her, including Mary, so she was a stranger to you all. I'm guessing that for whatever reason, she returned and wanted something from Arnold, most likely something to do with the child they had, but again nobody has ever met. It explains why the red boots were in the woods, doesn't it, Mary?"

Now it was Mary's turn to drain of all colour, and she turned from facing the door to me, eyes flashing with pure hate. "You don't know what you're talking about. Come on, Arnold, we're leaving."

"We can't, Mum, there are police at the door. I told you I should have owned up. It's over now, and I'm glad. I'm not a killer, and you shouldn't have done what you did. It just made things worse. I should have taken my punishment, and you should have left things well alone."

"Stop talking," she hissed, slapping him with her stick across his stomach.

Arnold winced, and as Mary pulled her arm back to hit him again, he snatched the stick from her thin arms and snapped it in half over a bony knee then threw the pieces to the floor.

The room gasped as the pieces clattered to the flagstones then rolled under a pew.

Mary wailed, but her posture changed from that of a frail elderly lady to a much more robust seeming woman with a ramrod straight back and an evil glare as she confronted her son and demanded, "You better say sorry. How dare you!? Now let's go."

"Nobody is going anywhere, Mary," said Monroe, glancing at his partner with utter shock at what was happening.

"You don't seriously believe this fool?" asked Mary.

"I want to hear what he has to say. Max and Min found a pair of child's red shoes in the woods at the campsite. Everyone but Min thought it meant nothing. Max, what's your take on this?"

"I assumed someone had just found them then left them there, but the more I thought about it, and the more I heard about Arnold having been married but that he never brought his wife here, the more I began to think. Maybe he had a child and maybe Mary had brought that child a present. After Arnold and his wife split up, she refused to visit with the child and wouldn't let either Mary or Arnold see the baby. Mary likes to leave offerings, and always lays flowers and sweet trinkets at her husband's grave, and little things dotted around town for friends or family who have passed, and it got me to thinking about the way the boots were hung up. She always used to love walking up in the woods, so I'm guessing it was her who left them there as a way of remembering the child that although not dead, was as good as dead to her and Arnold. Am I wrong?" I asked her.

"Of course you are. What nonsense?"

"Is there a child, Mary?" asked Monroe. "We never quite believed it."

Mary shook her head but didn't speak.

"Yes, there is," admitted Arnold. "My beautiful baby boy born ten years ago, and I never once got to see him. Taylor kicked me out when he was almost due, got the police involved, and got a restraining order against me. They took her side, even though I explained it was an accident when I hit her. She gave birth and refused to let me have anything to do with the child. Mum tried and tried to get her to see sense, but she refused. I didn't know about the boots in the woods. Mum said she threw them out. You put them there, didn't you?"

"Stop talking," growled Mary. "You're being a foolish boy. Just keep quiet."

"I will not. This is all you fault. You should have let me admit it when it happened. But oh no, you had to interfere like always, and you made it so much worse. I'm a bad man and deserve to be punished, but so do you. You did a terrible thing, Mum. Terrible."

"What are we saying here?" asked Karl.

Arnold hung his head. Mary glared at me.

"Arnold killed his ex-wife, but Mary killed Hayley. I'm right, aren't I?"

"Yes," whispered Arnold, his voice low but the church so quiet that you could hear a pin drop.

"Stop talking!" Mary swung for Arnold, but he caught her fist easily.

"No more hitting. You've done it your whole life. I never went a day when I was little without having a bruise I had to hide. I could never play sports, or have any friends, because you turned me into a weak, scared, friendless child. Oh, you were great at hiding it in public and nobody else ever knew, apart from Dad, but you made my life miserable. I thought it was normal, although deep down I knew it wasn't, and when I lashed out at Taylor she showed me what it really means to hit someone and the consequences. You ruined my marriage, ruined my life, and now it might as well be over. I'm going to tell everyone everything."

"Enough!" demanded Mary, but she deflated and her defiance softened. "I'm so sorry. It's just my way. How I was brought up. If a child's naughty, they deserve to be punished. That's what I was taught. Maybe all of this is for the best."

"Mary," asked Karl, "did you put the boots in the woods?"

"Yes. I knew I would never see my grandson. Taylor made that more than clear. I'd bought them months before the child was born and was excited to see my grandson, but then everything went sour and I have never seen the child."

"And where is that child now?" asked Karl "You are both saying that the deceased woman was Taylor, Arnold's wife?"

"Yes, it was her," confirmed Arnold. "My son is with his grandparents. Taylor came because I called her and told her I had come into money and wanted to give it to her for young Pete. I'm sorry, Natasha, about her tying you up, and to you Max and Min for ruining your wedding, but I made her do it."

"Why? That's the one thing I don't understand. Why did you get her to attack Natasha and pretend to be her? I can't figure it out."

"I can!" shouted Min as she stood. "Arnold told her she had to do it if she wanted the money."

"But why?" asked Swede, as caught up in the drama as everyone else.

"So she could get a taste of her own medicine, right?" Min asked Arnold.

"Yes. I wasn't thinking straight, but when she arrived and was really mean to me, I wanted her to suffer a little. Of course, there was no money, but I wanted to see her and hoped she'd bring Pete along. She didn't, and I got angry. I told her she'd have to ruin someone else's marriage, like she ruined ours. I told her I was sorry when I hit her, but that wasn't enough. So I made her tie up the vicar and go and do your ceremony. She's a very religious person and knew how weddings worked as she was always dragging me along to one of her friend's weddings, and she agreed, but wasn't happy about it."

"So you made her do it just to ruin things for us?" I asked, surprised by such a ridiculous thing to do and how petty it was.

"Not just that. We heard about the wedding that was about to happen and it just came to me that I could get her to do something that I knew she would hate. That went against her morals. I proved it to her, didn't I? I proved that she wasn't as nice as she acted after all. She'd sacrifice her beliefs, do something terrible to two people who were happy, and all for money. She wasn't a good woman."

"And then you killed her?" I asked.

"She called me, said she didn't go through with it and made an excuse about her allergies. I saw red and used Mum's new poker and killed her at the church where she was about to tell Natasha everything and get me into trouble. I couldn't let her do that. Mum would have been so disappointed in me. I didn't even realise I was holding the poker until I attacked Taylor. I must have picked it up when I was really angry and just rushed to the church where we argued, then I did it."

"But that wasn't the end of things, was it?" I asked softly, hoping he'd explain the rest. "Hayley must have seen you do it and maybe overheard about the money. And why the ribbon in Taylor's mouth? Had you bought a gift for your son?"

"Yes, a gift. A cute teddy bear I'd been holding on to for years. She laughed at me, said she'd never give it to Pete. I stuffed it into her mouth but left the bear on Dad's grave."

"And Hayley? She saw what you did?"

Arnold tugged at the fur on the parka's hood and nodded. "She was a nasty woman. She didn't care that Taylor was dead, but she demanded I give her the money instead or she'd tell the police. I agreed to keep her quiet, but when I told Mum what I'd done, she said she'd deal with it. I thought Mum was going to pay her off, but you didn't, did you?"

"I don't have any money, you fool!"

"Stop talking to me like that! Stop making me feel bad about myself. No wonder I turned out how I did with you never saying a kind word or doing anything nice with me. This is all your fault!"

"I never realised," murmured Mary. "It's just my way. I had to do it, don't you see?" she pleaded, arms out, talking directly to everyone. "Hayley would have told on my boy and he'd be in big trouble. He's all I have in the world. I love him."

"You do?" asked Arnold, eyes rising.

"Of course."

"Then why didn't you ever tell me that?" he wailed, then sank to his knees, a broken, defeated man.

Mary stroked his head, both of them now lost to their own world. "You're my everything. I had to kill Hayley as she would have told once she knew there was no money. It was easy to take the poker to the pub, and when she went down to the river like we'd arranged, I got rid of her for you. For us."

"I think we've heard enough," said Monroe. "Take them away. Get them out of here," he told the officers who were already halfway down the aisle and poised.

Arnold was helped to his feet, then he and Mary were led away, the church utterly silent apart from Mary's quiet sobbing. Arnold didn't say a word, or make eye-contact with anyone.

The door closed with a lingering creak.

"Someone should oil those hinges," said Dad merrily, winking at me, the pride evident.

"That was…" began Karl.

"Interesting," finished Monroe. "The poor man lost the plot, but with a mother like that it's hardly surprising. Been beaten his whole life and never knew a mother's love or how to act in the world. That's one messed-up guy."

"Mary was always such a lovely lady. A little forgetful, and a bit too loose with her cane, but she always seemed so nice." Phil rubbed at his head and sighed, frowning.

"She fooled everyone," said Swede. "So are we saying that she didn't lose her shopping or her poker like she said?"

"Of course she didn't. It was a ruse," said Phil. "She pretended they'd been nicked so nobody would suspect her lad was involved in the killing."

"Yeah, I know that! I get it." Swede squared his shoulders, clearly hating being made to look like he hadn't been following events, then asked, "So Arnold never got to see his own boy? That's awful."

"Why should he?" demanded a woman I'd never seen before. "He didn't deserve to have a child."

The place erupted into a cacophony of shouting, arguing, insults, sympathising, and general astonishment as most people stood, unsure what to do now. I caught Min's eye and she mouthed a silent, "Are you okay?" and I nodded, relieved it was all over and that I hadn't got things completely wrong. I'd been confident, but standing in front of everyone and knowing how important this was had made me doubt my own mind. I knew it made sense, that somebody had to have known the mystery woman, but the reason why she was forced to impersonate the vicar was still a shock. To have done that just to make Taylor break her moral code was petty and mean.

"Another one for the wiki page," hollered Dad above the din. "And I can tell everyone that I helped figure it out."

"No, you didn't," declared Mum. "If anything, it was me who helped. I'm the one who, er, um…" For once, Mum was lost for words, and I couldn't help smiling despite the circumstance, pleased that some things would never change.

"Time for us to go, Anxious," I told him, bending to give him a fuss. "You behaved so well, and I'm very proud of you. Don't let the others know, but really it was you who solved these crimes."

Anxious cocked his head, one eye on my pocket, the other on me.

I laughed as I pulled out a biscuit; he inhaled it before looking back at me.

"Without you finding those little offerings Mary left in various places, I don't think things would have clicked into place like they did, so well done."

Anxious barked his agreement, then suddenly jumped up, ran to a still astonished Natasha, and pawed gently at her leg before turning to me and barking. Then he ran back over to me, barked again, before dashing down the aisle and yipping at Min.

"Quiet, everyone, the dog's got something to say," shouted Dad as he grinned like he'd won the lottery.

Incredibly, everyone obeyed, and the church fell silent as Anxious gently tugged at Min's sandal, pulling her down the aisle towards me.

Min smiled at me, and I understood immediately what Anxious had wanted, and what she seemed to be expecting.

"Min?" I asked.

"I spoke to Natasha earlier, and she said that she could do it after the service if we wanted. I know it's rather unconventional, but I wasn't expecting you to reveal the killers when I asked her, but why not? I know it's not how we wanted it to happen, but we are here, and a church wedding would be nice."

"Isn't it in bad taste to get married right after we've unearthed two killers, and in a church?" I asked, my smile spreading.

"I think it's a wonderful idea," said Natasha. "Min and I spoke earlier and I told her that it would be my honour to finally get you two wed. Yes, that was all rather a shock, but I don't see why such a terrible thing can't finish with a happy ending. Does anyone here object?"

"Go for it!" shouted Swede.

"Good on ya," called out Phil.

"I'm his mother," roared Mum, puffing out her chest. "That's my boy!"

"And mine," called out Dad, hurtling down the aisle as people took their seats.

"Let's do this!" I shouted, grabbing Min around the waist and twirling her.

"And are you happy to get married in front of all these people?" asked Natasha.

Min and I nodded to each other, then I told Natasha, "We feel like we're already part of this community, so if nobody objects?"

Nobody did, so with Anxious cradled in my arms, Mum, Dad, Uncle Ernie, and a beaming Moose standing to the side, Natasha stood facing the congregation and without fuss, began the wedding ceremony.

In a daze of happiness, several minutes later I gasped, "I do," my heart leaping for joy as finally my world was complete. Natasha pronounced us man and wife and said I could kiss Min, so feeling like the happiest man on earth, that's exactly what I did.

My folks, Ernie, and Moose congratulated us, the pride shining on their smiling faces, then the whole church erupted into a raucous round of applause. Bashful but ecstatic, we turned and said thank you.

My phone rang, so I pulled it out, noted the caller ID, then put my finger to my lips as I answered. Everyone fell silent as I said, "Hi, you're on loudspeaker. Can you tell me why you're calling please so everyone can hear? We're in church, and just got married."

"Um, hi, Max, it's Carl from the campsite. Firstly, congratulations, and secondly, I'd like to confirm that we accept your offer. The campsite is yours if you want it."

I turned to Min, eyebrow raised, and asked, "Well? A new start, a place to call home, but we can stay in Vee as long as we want. What do you think?"

"Oh, Max. Yes. Absolutely yes!"

"Did you hear that, Carl? The answer is yes."

"I heard. Congratulations on the marriage, and for being the new owners of Craven Oaks Campsite. Speak soon."

Grinning from ear to ear, hardly able to contain myself, I whispered into Min's ear, "This isn't the end. This is a new beginning. A new series of adventures."

We embraced as our new community applauded while Mum, Dad, and Uncle Ernie vied over who would hug us first—Mum won, obviously! Finally, our dream had come true. We had our whole lives ahead of us, and were together again at last. This time, we would remain that way.

The End

p.s. We ended up having leftover beef stew on our wedding night, and it was lovely. For once, I had other things on my mind besides cooking!

It's not quite the end though. As Max said, it's just the beginning. Before we get into that, read on for an incredible one-pot wonder. You will also find a link to a free cookbook containing all 15 recipes from the series as a way of saying thank you for getting this far.

Recipe

Paella for Four

This is my paella, inauthentic and proud! To be honest, practically every Spanish village will tell you their paella is the best and the only genuine version of Spain's national dish. So if mine isn't quite how José in Paüls would make it, that's okay.

This is made with my preferred mix of vegetables, meat, and seafood, but of course you can mix this up to use whatever you have to hand. The only real must haves are proper paella rice. Super flavour absorbing short grains from Spain please, and saffron. Paella isn't paella without those two. If I was feeling particularly preachy, I'd suggest only ever using Bomba grains from the Ebro Delta, but that is perhaps a step too far.

To be authentic, we'd be cooking this over wood and won't stir the rice to ensure a smokey crust is formed on the base of the paella pan. This is the all important flavourful socarrat. However, things can get trickier with a smaller heat source, so you may want to spin the pan around every so often to ensure it is heated evenly, or you can go rogue and stir the rice every now and then. You'll lose the smokey crust, but it might be less stressful.

You will need a large shallow pan around 30cm across if you don't have a paella pan.

Ingredients

- Olive oil - a good few lugs
- Boneless, skinless chicken thighs - 4, roughly chopped
- Raw chorizo - 75g sliced
- Garlic - 3 cloves crushed
- Onion - 1 medium finely diced

- Red pepper - 1 diced
- Green pepper - 1 diced
- Chopped tomatoes - 400g tin
- Saffron - a good pinch
- Sweet smoked paprika - 1tsp
- Salt - 1tsp
- Paella rice - 300g
- Chicken or vegetable stock - 1 litre
- Raw jumbo prawns - shell on - 8 (at least)
- Flat green beans - 100g, chopped
- Frozen peas - 100g
- Lemon wedges - 4

Method

- Heat the olive oil on a medium heat before adding the chorizo, chicken, and onion. Cook for ten minutes or so, stirring regularly.
- Once the chorizo has started to give up some of its fabulous red fat, add the garlic and peppers. Cook for another five minutes, stirring to get everything glossy.
- Add the tomatoes and cook on a low heat for ten to fifteen minutes to reduce down. Season with salt, saffron, and paprika.
- Pop in the rice, and turn the heat up to high. Fry, stirring, for two minutes before adding around 2/3 of the stock.
- Once things are bubbly, turn the heat down and cook slowly for twenty minutes. You can add a little more stock if you think it's getting a little too dry. Be careful not to burn it! This is where you may wish to turn your pan to ensure the whole thing is heated evenly.

- Sprinkle over the beans and peas before arranging your prawns in an even layer. Top with some foil and continue cooking on a medium high heat for another five minutes until the prawns are pink and opaque and the rice is cooked, but still with a little bit of bite.
- Take the pan off the heat and allow it to rest for a further ten minutes.
- Serve with lemon wedges and plenty of ice-cold cava (that's not negotiable!).

Bon profit!

From the Author

Thank you so much for reading the series. I can't even begin to tell you how much fun it's been. I've had a blast writing these stories, and have grown to love Max, Min, Anxious (who, let's face it, is the real star), and his bonkers parents.

In fact, I love them so much that I want to find out what happens next. Maybe you do too? Then let's begin a new series of adventures together. Grab the first in the new series called Max's Campsite Mysteries, and read The Campsite Cadaver to see what's in store for our favourite couple now they've decided to renovate the campsite. I have a sneaking suspicion that it won't go smoothly, but let's see, shall we?

You can also follow me on Amazon www.amazon.com/stores/author/B0BN6T2VQ5 to find out when the new season is released.

Once again, thank you so much for following along with Max and the gang, and for all the words of encouragement on Facebook and via email. It's truly incredible how kind everyone has been, and without you, dear reader, none of this would be possible.

As a big thank you for all your support I would like to offer you a free cookbook containing all of Max's recipes in one handy place. You can also buy the paperback if you wish, although, obviously, it's far from a large book. Have fun with the one-pot wonders!

FREE: Max's One-Pot Wonders Digital Edition - www.authortylerrhodes.com/maxs-one-pot-wonders/

Get the Paperback Edition at www.amazon.co.uk/Maxs-One-Pot-Wonders-Delicious-Campervan/dp/B0FHPS8ZJ4/

Be sure to stay updated about new releases and fan sales. You'll hear about them first. No spam, just book updates at www.authortylerrhodes.com.

Connect with me on Facebook www.facebook.com/authortylerrhodes/